THE WARM DOG DAYS OF SUMMER WERE NOW UPON THEM,
AND JUBEE AND MARGARET WERE TAKING TEA IN A GAZEBO.

THE WONDERFUL EDISON TIME MACHINE

A Celebration of Life

by

MALCOLM WILLITS

Hypostyle Hall
PUBLISHERS

Published in the United States of America by
Hypostyle Hall, 6225 Hollywood Boulevard, Hollywood, California 90028
Phone 323-467-9459   FAX 323-467-4536

Printed in the United States of America by

The Castle Press
1222 North Fair Oaks Avenue, Pasadena, California 91103

Project Director — Craig Woods
Color Separations — Richard Warrick

Bound in the United States of America

Set in Adobe Garamond Book

Printed on 80 pound Mohawk Superfine White

Except for certain historical personages and long-established institutions mentioned in
THE WONDERFUL EDISON TIME MACHINE, the novel's story and characters are fictitious.

Grateful acknowledgement is made to the following
for permission to reprint lyrics from previously published material:

"TOMORROW"
Lyrics by Martin Charnin
©1977 EDWIN H. MORRIS & COMPANY
A DIVISION OF
MPL COMMUNICATION, INC.
USED BY PERMISSION

"THE JAPANESE SANDMAN" — lyrics by Raymond B. Egan, music by Richard A. Whiting ©1920
"SONNY BOY" — words and music by Al Jolson ©1928
"CRAZY WORDS, CRAZY TUNE" — music by Milton Ager, lyrics by Jack Yellen
"LEAVE IT TO JANE" — music by Jerome Kern, lyrics by PG Wodehouse
"SMILES" — by Lee S. Roberts, lyrics by J. Will Callahan ©1917, renewed 1941

Every effort has been made to identify and locate the copyright proprietors
and secure permission to reproduce the lyrics from the songs listed above.

FIRST EDITION

Library of Congress Catalogue Card Number: 99-96504

ISBN 0-9675253-0-6

Book design
by
C.W. SCOTT RUBEL
Fine Paper Company
Pasadena, California

Illustrated

by

Toby

Dedicated to

Michael Moore

and the

Intrepid Citizens

of

Flint, Michigan

CONTENTS

PROLOGUE

Once upon a time, in the city of Flint, Michigan, there was a place of occasional higher learning called Central High School. It was located on Crapo Street, a seedy thoroughfare named in better times for William Crapo Durant, the founder of General Motors. But the factories he'd built and the cars that rolled from them were long since gone, and even the impassioned resident who filmed the people's desperate plight had long since left for better climes. So the students in this penitential place pronounced the street name differently, and vowed to anyone who'd listen that God had clearly crapped on them.

Our tale begins on a particularly dull and listless day when desultory singing could be heard emanating from the high school auditorium. Its off-key tentacles curled like a pestilence down weathered stairs and echoed in the halls of broken lockers. It seeped through ill-fitting doors and unwashed windows out into the empty courtyard, where merciful winds carried it away.

The culprit was the Drama Club. It had exhumed a 1920s collegiate musical called "Leave It to Jane," and was offering it as its annual onslaught on the arts to an audience of several hundred somnolent students in various

The Wonderful Edison Time Machine

stages of numbness and despair. They were guarded by their wardens, whose contracts called them teachers, all of whom had wondered, in the wee small hours of some troubled dawn, where their lives had gone wrong.

Outside, in the empty hallway, a door clicked shut, and heavy breathing could be heard on some back stairs. A door opened a nitch. Revealed was a backstage dressing area, where a group of boys in various stages of dress were preparing to go on stage. Several blankets partitioned them from a comparable group of girls just beyond.

A curtain moved unnoticed, and a raccoon coat was taken. A pair of white striped trousers disappeared, only to reappear as a student looked for them. Absently, he nodded thanks, while another pair behind him slipped away. Another student checked his makeup in a mirror, two 1920s hats nearby. He slicked his hair and reached for one. Both were gone.

A shirt edged across a bench as a student reached for it. A tug-of-war ensued. A foot came from beneath the curtain and kicked the boy. He let it go with an oath, and others looked toward the commotion.

Two more costumes disappeared, and several boys charged over. A hidden hand untied a rope.

On stage, the scenery collapsed in confusion, revealing the dressing area and its fleeing thespians frantically trying to cover their immodesty. The audience came alive with raucous jeers and laughter. A boy rushed out clad only in his underwear, pointing stage left.

"I saw who did it. It was those awful..."

A falling backdrop sent him reeling to the floor. Pandemonium broke out, and the condemned made a massive jailbreak for the door. Two girls fanning a fainted teacher were trampled in the exodus, while one boy paused to take her purse. Unknown assailants took the opportunity to familiarize themselves with previously unassailable females, and when they all spilled out into the corridor, it was like a dam had burst at Devil's Island.

If heaven had been watching, surely bells would have been rung. For the

PROLOGUE

perpetrators of this panic were now racing pell-mell across the schoolground. Their arms were covered with the stolen garments, and they laughed uproariously at the sky. They were Jubee, Spiff and Dud, the unlikely heroes of our story, whose names had long ago been elevated by a succession of vice-principals to Central High School's honor roll of shame.

They ran joyfully through the desolate and abandoned sections of the city of Flint. They dodged some cars while bums looked on. They cut across a junk-filled lot where a tattered sign showed a new but mundane automobile. It read "Ossified Motors — Big as a Dinosaur — If You Liked Our Cars Last Year, You'll Like Them This Year Too." It displayed a trademark silhouette of a dinosaur.

The boys ran past a rundown house where a family was piling its few possessions onto a dilapidated truck, then past a cemetery of abandoned American cars. Ahead of them, two crooks were backing out of a liquor store. The boys collided with them as the Vietnamese owners came rushing out. The sounds of battle raged behind them as the boys continued on. They finally entered a better part of town and disappeared beyond an impressive billboard that included the words "No Crock: It's a Krockashita" and showed a painting of a fine new car with Mt. Fujiyama in the background.

*   *   *   *   *

Night came to the city of Flint like a salesman's folded suitcase and cast its benevolence on row after row of working-class homes. One of them was Dud's, and this evening found him in his upstairs room. He was a big and awkward lad, not too bright, but dog-like in his devotion and comprehension. Dressed in his stolen 1920s garb, complete even to a college pennant and ukelele tied to a belt loop, he was finishing tying up a sleeping bag. He then unflapped a cardboard box, revealing a large quantity of brightly-colored Jujubes candy boxes. He opened a nearby sack and transferred even more boxes of Jujubes. He then took up the sleeping bag and carton of candy, and left the room.

Downstairs, his father, clad in his undershirt, sat heavily in front of a TV set. He was surrounded by empty beer bottles, and his unseen wife was yammering at him from the kitchen.

"So why all of a sudden you don't like ravioli? Your grandmother, she give me the recipe. Your mother, she say..."

Her voice was lost in that of the announcer's, who intoned over scenes of fighting:

"The impending sale of Ossified Motors to a Japanese consortium continues to dominate the news. In a near riot this afternoon, a group of Flint citizens, concerned about the effect the plant's closure would have on the local economy, were turned back from the factory's gates by a phalanx of armed security guards."

Dud had now reached the bottom of the stairs. His father gazed at his 1920s outfit, then looked at the bottle of beer he was holding as his son made for the door.

Jubee was also actively at work. A handsome boy, he too was dressed in his stolen garments, and was watching his Apple computer equipment wind down in his well-appointed room. He folded a final printout in his notebook, then grabbed his sleeping bag. He looked around his room as if he'd be gone for a long time, and then walked out, passing an Hispanic maid putting away linens. From an adjoining room, his little brother saw him leave.

Spiff was a black boy, and the remaining member of our unholy trio. He was similarly dressed and was furtively opening a chest of drawers. He removed a large old photo album and, with eyes kept warily on the door, carefully opened it. He turned to a portrait of a black man in prison uniform holding a number. Beneath it was written "Big Jim Birdsong, 1883-1945." Beside it was an embedded gold coin, which Spiff quickly removed and pocketed. He then picked up a nearby roll of blankets and departed.

The boy was halfway down the stairs when there came a mocking female voice: "My, ain't you the cat's pajamas."

Spiff slammed the door and went out into the night.

CHAPTER ONE

THE ADVENTURE BEGINS

They met on a wide and empty road where the stars seemed close and watchful. The hour was late, and the single ancient street lamp made shadows longer than themselves. The boys stood before the broken gates of a secluded estate with unkept trees and an abandoned mansion that loomed broodingly above. Jubee was the first to speak, and he spoke in whispers.

"It's about time! Did you bring the candy?"

Dud sighed and indicated that he had.

Spiff eyed their surroundings with a rising apprehension. "Can we really go in there?" he asked.

"Of course we can," said Jubee. "My great aunt lives here."

"Why doesn't she leave any lights on?" inquired Dud.

"She goes to bed early. She's sort of weird."

"What's her name?"

"Mad Margaret."

Spiff had his own private cow at this revelation, but the others did not notice.

"Just be quiet so we don't wake her up."

With this admonition, Jubee and his two friends slipped inside and stealthily crossed the ruined driveway, taking pains to skirt the mansion. Spiff mostly looked backward. He had been out this late before on nocturnal hubcap-hunting expeditions, but this place made him nervous. He would have been more nervous if he had looked up and seen the withered hand that parted a tattered curtain in an upstairs window of the house.

The boys approached an out-building which had once been the chauffeur's quarters. Jubee stopped by a doorway and fished a key from a nearby can. He gingerly worked the lock.

"Are you sure it's inside here?" said Dud. The still, cold night was beginning to get to him as well.

"Sure I'm sure," said Jubee grimly.

"What if she wakes up? What if she thinks we're burglars?" Spiff said. He liked to be prepared for any eventuality, whereas Dud would merely fight his way out of anything that happened.

"She sleeps like a dog," Jubee assured him, just as the rusty lock broke loose. "C'mon."

Behind them in the mansion, two arms covered in a nightdress reached for a shotgun on a wall. Oblivious to this, the boys entered a ghostly hallway, and with the aid of a flashlight climbed some nearby stairs. Above was another hallway, this one crowded with trunks and shrouded furniture. A few steps down, Jubee carefully opened a side door. The others entered with him, and Dud flashed his light around.

"Wait a second," said Jubee. He lit a lamp and a mellow light infused the long-forgotten room. "It's over here," he said. "I covered it with boxes."

He moved a few steps further and then began to move a number of boxes and old baskets as his friends watched curiously. Within moments a bulky object covered with a moldy quilt came into view. With a flourish Jubee threw off the cover, revealing a genuine 1910 EDISON TIME MACHINE.

Spiff and Dud were awestruck. "WOW! It's *beautiful*. It looks so *old*."

"It's a real Edison Time Machine," said Jubee proudly. "Made in 1910. I polished it myself."

"Can it *really* take us back into the past?" gasped Spiff.

"Back to 1929, anyway."

THE BOYS STOOD BEFORE THE BROKEN GATES OF A SECLUDED ESTATE WITH UNKEMPT TREES AND
AN ABANDONED MANSION THAT LOOMED BROODINGLY ABOVE.

THE ADVENTURE BEGINS

Dud was always practical. "Why can't we go back farther? I'd like to meet King Arthur. If Edison was so smart, why did he invent a Time Machine that can't go back very far?"

"I *told* you," Jubee said. "His machine can only go back into its *own* past. That's why it can only go back as far as 1910, because that's when Edison invented it."

"Then why can't we go into the future?" argued Dud. "I'd like to see if Windy Hesperus has children as ugly as she is. Because if she does, I don't want to marry her." Spiff laughed.

"We can't go into the future because the machine hasn't existed in the future. It's only existed until today. So we can only go in one direction — *back!*"

At that very moment a beam from a penlight was advancing across the ground. It could have only one meaning — TROUBLE was on the way.

Spiff was smarter than people gave him credit for. "Wait a minute. If the Time Machine can only go into the past, how are we going to get *back*? If we're in 1929 and want to get back to 1991, we've got to travel…sixty-two years into the future. But you say it won't go into the future."

"That's right," responded Jubee. "But the machine is really going *back* into its past to pick us up. *We* may be going forward, but the *machine* is only going back into its own past. Here, I'll show you."

[5]

THE WONDERFUL EDISON TIME MACHINE

The beam of light was mounting the very stairs the boys had used.

Jubee opened the mahogany doors of the Time Machine and pointed to some old-fashioned numerals. "I've already set the dials. See here: 'Arrival Date in the Past' to May 5, 1929. That's a Sunday. Things should be quiet, and we'll have a chance to get our bearings. And here: 'Departure Date in the Past.' We're returning on November second. We'll be six months in 1929. Then the machine will automatically bring us back to 1991."

"Why 1929?" asked Dud. "You promised to tell us before we left."

Outside the door, the penlight beam had stopped. Somebody knew the boys were there, and that somebody was listening.

Jubee had told the story so many times it was engraved upon his heart. But he embarked on it again, for what he hoped would be the last time.

"You *know* my family used to own the Wizzer Automobile Company. We made millions of cars, back in the 1920s. We were rich, really rich. And that house out there was the family mansion, with servants everywhere. It's all I've heard about since I was small. Then in 1929 we lost it all. And we've been poor as church mice ever since."

Spiff snorted at this bogus claim to poverty.

"So what can *we* do about it?" demanded Dud.

"We can find out what happened and prevent it. That way the Wizzer Automobile Company will stay in the family and I'll be born *rich*."

"That would take a ton of money. Even in 1929," reflected Spiff.

"We'll *have* a ton of money." Jubee smiled broadly. "I've got it all figured out." He moved toward the waiting Time Machine, and the others followed. Dud asked how it worked.

Jubee raised the shutter of the machine. "You just put on an Edison phonograph record — he invented the phonograph, you know — wind it up (he wound a handle vigorously) and turn it on."

"A wind-up Time Machine," thought Spiff, agog.

Just at that moment there came a ghostly voice from outside the room.

THE ADVENTURE BEGINS

"Woo-ooo-ooo!"

The boys froze.

"WOO-OOO-OOO." It came again, and louder.

There was a frantic search for hiding places. Jubee blew out the lamp, and all was still. The door then opened and a pint-sized figure covered with a sheet entered the room. A flashlight was upended inside to illuminate a ghastly and misshapen face.

"Woo-ooo-ooo," the specter again said in a sepulchral voice. "I am the ghost of Christmas past."

"W-what do you want?" cried Spiff and Dud. "Go away!"

But Jubee, with his wits intact, sprang forward. "I *know* this ghost," he said, and quickly uncovered the figure. Revealed was his younger brother, Lucian.

"LUCIFER!" said Spiff and Dud in unison.

"That's *Lucian*," corrected Lucian, not liking the name that all applied to him.

"What are *you* doing here?" demanded his older brother.

"I know you're up to something," said the little boy. "So I followed you. I want to be rich too. Take me with you or I'll tell Mom and Dad."

"Go ahead," said Jubee, used to his brother's attempts at blackmail. "Besides, you haven't got a sleeping bag."

"I do, too," responded Lucian. "It's outside in the hall." He scampered outside to get it, and Jubee slammed and locked the door. He then leaped to the Time Machine and turned it on.

"We'll be gone before the runt can get back in."

There was a moment of silence; then a pounding at the door. "Let me in. Let me *in!*" cried Lucian.

The older boys laughed at the continued pounding, but then it stopped, followed by an eerie silence. Then came a panic-stricken voice.

"Someone's coming. Oh, God! Someone's coming down the hall. LET ME

THE WONDERFUL EDISON TIME MACHINE

IN! *PLEASE!* IT'S GOT A GUN. IT'S COMING CLOSER, IT'S GOING TO GET ME. *HELP!*" And he began to cry.

"Imaginative little peck—" said Jubee, but his words were shortened by the deafening blast of a shotgun. Jubee yanked the door open and pulled his brother inside.

"HOLY SHIT!" he said.

"It's *Mad Margaret!*" cried Dud and Spiff. "Why didn't you put her in a nursing home? What'll we do? WHAT'LL WE DO?"

All four boys began frantically piling boxes against the door. Behind them, unnoticed, the Time Machine was beginning to glow with life. With it came the first faint sounds of "The Japanese Sandman."

There came another shotgun blast, this one through the door. It was followed by a maniacal laugh.

Behind them the Time Machine had become translucent. Two antennas emerged, each with oddly-shaped bulbs that revolved in opposite directions. A bubble-like field began extending outward as it slowly elevated and began to rotate.

The blade of an ax now penetrated the door, and the boys retreated, horror-stricken. Again there came the laugh, and Jubee cried in terror: "Aunt Meg! It's me! Your nephew, Wentworth!"

"We're your *relatives*," wailed Spiff.

The door was rent anew. Behind them the Time Machine rotated faster, its multi-colored bubble advancing further into the room. The "Sandman" music was louder now. Unaware, the boys fell to their knees and covered their faces. Swiftly the bubble engulfed them in its swirling light.

The last ax blow destroyed the door. Withered hands tore away its few remaining fragments. The music was winding down, and the wondrous light had all but disappeared. Mad Margaret, a spectral woman of 77 years, forced her demented face through the opening. Her final laugh was cut short when she saw the room was silent and unoccupied. The Time Machine had settled to a rest, and its lights, once coals of fire, had cooled and gone out. The boys, the sleeping bags, the box of candy — all were gone.

* * * * *

They were in a tunnel filled with wind. It came at them with the force of a tornado, and they clung to one another in fear and desperation. Glowing years advanced like railway trains, and the "Sandman" music now had a mocking sound, as if coming from a carnival in Hell.

1989, 1987, 1983; the years enveloped them and then receded. 1963, 1956, 1944; and with them smokey scenes of war and desolation. A field of bodies with numbed survivors bleak as crows, a city gone in a single flash, battleships ablaze in a tropic paradise, tanks mired on a plain of death. And always, soldiers marching to oblivion.

The years were coming faster now: 1937,1934, 1932; breadlines, sit-down strikes, sullen armies of the unemployed. Cops with clubs, and wraith-like figures departing farms condemned by God. Factories closed and shuttered, their smokeless chimneys pointing skyward in unheard supplication. It was a land seemed blasted, its youth adrift on endless roads through hostile, hollow towns.

THE WONDERFUL EDISON TIME MACHINE

But now the light had brightened, the years were slowing down, and it was 1929. December, November, October; it was as if a subway train was coasting into station. The "Sandman" music returned to normal — Al Jolson could be seen on bended knee, and Lucky Lindy on a flying tour. People danced the Charleston, wayward flappers waved from rumble seats, and Babe Ruth bowed to fans in Yankee Stadium.

September, August, July — gangsters strutted on the streets, jazz-mad crowds filled speakeasies, and flagpole sitters sat aloft in splendid isolation. Then came May, followed by the days: 29, 27, 19, 18, and they slowed to a hissing sound like steam escaping as happy throngs passed rich store windows and crossed streets to a cacophony of bleating cars.

And as the music ended, the magic numbers stopped at 5. Everything went blank, and there came a thumping sound, like four sacks of potatoes dumped onto a floor.

The boys had arrived in Oz!

CHAPTER TWO

THE NEVER-ENDING PARTY

The boys were in the same room, but the junk was now more orderly. Sprawled haphazardly, they groggily came to. Behind them the Time Machine in 1929, dusty and tarnished, was settling to its final turn.

Holding their heads, the boys struggled to their feet and looked around. Much seemed the same, and yet… They approached the door with caution. It was unlocked and showed no sign of damage. They opened it and stepped into the hall. It was more changed, and lighter. Together they crept down the stairs. Now they could hear the sound of voices. They advanced to the door, opened it, and stared out into the evening.

The mansion was aglow with light. Party sounds flowed from every room, and a jazz band was playing "The Japanese Sandman." Hundreds of people were milling on the lawn and fluttering like moths along the shadowed pathways lined with paper lanterns. Hedonistic lovers splashed in the pool, and the air itself seemed perfumed with the scent of youth and beauty.

"If this is Sunday," Jubee marveled, "I wonder what their Saturdays are like."

As in a dream, the boys walked past a stream of huge, luxurious cars with hoods that seemed a mile long and motors that pulsated with a rhythmic power and throbbed to be unleashed. From them stepped revelers in a riot of costumes from every age in history who already seemed intoxicated with the night and with themselves.

With trepidation, the boys mounted the steps which led into the house.

THE WONDERFUL EDISON TIME MACHINE

Here the terrace doors were open, and they saw the scene inside. Hundreds more were dancing in the ballroom. Flappers cavorted on top of a grand piano, while vamps and sheiks and tuxedoed millionaires chased their favorite phantoms among the palms and statuary. All the while, liveried servants plied the crowd with food from trays of delicacies, and the scene itself was like some *ancien régime* on the eve of revolution.

Like visitors from another world, the boys continued on through other rooms, each more frantic than the one before. Unbeknownst to them, they became part of a growing pilgrimage winding its way toward the grand staircase and the silver fountain on its landing which beckoned like a shrine. It was topped by a figure of Bacchus and surrounded by a multitude of emerald spigots from which flowed the finest wines and liquors the world had to offer. Flush with the treasures of the earth, the golden people approached with reverence and lost themselves in its sparkling libations.

It was here an attendant spotted them. "You boys are not in costume," he announced, and led them to a nearby room where maids, scurrying among racks of brilliant clothing, looked at them with interest. They were led to a dressing booth where, to their cries of indignation, they were stripped almost to the buff. Even as their clothes sailed over the top, mirrors were brought in and their measurements were taken. Sketches were considered, and soon a line of servants entered, their arms piled high with clothing. When they emerged, they were disheveled but triumphant.

Dud was the first to step out. He was dressed as a Spanish conquistador in silver armor and an inky velvet doublet. Next to appear was Spiff, a desert Sheik of Araby with gleaming leather boots and flowing cape. Next came Jubee as an incandescent French aristocrat, a scented handkerchief in his upheld, haughty hand. And finally came Lucian, happy in his war paint, beaded Indian outfit and quiver filled with rubber arrows.

Now properly attired, the boys continued on, lost in the sea of festivities. A chef carved them succulents from a table groaning with the weight of food.

THE NEVER-ENDING PARTY

Later a saucy lass served them frosty mugs of root beer while they rested by some potted ferns. Jubee's eyes surveyed the crowd and he observed a gawky girl in her mid-20s feeding grapes and making goo-goo eyes at an anemic British lord. Farther on, a man was watching them. He was dirty from the sweat of honest labor and seemed out of place in the swirling, madcap crowd. He gazed at the girl in hopeless love, then turned around and left.

Later, in a night that knew no time, Spiff and Jubee were standing by two closed sliding doors. Jubee was now absorbed in thought. Lucian was a few steps away, perched on a chair and shooting arrows at the dancers. He reached for another one, but found his quiver empty. He spied one of his suction-cup arrows attached to the rear end of a nearby society matron who was doing an energetic rhumba. He jumped to the dance floor and made a grab for it, but missed. The little boy was forced to assume the dance steps in hopes of approaching her again, but each time he did so the music changed and he was spun away.

The orchestra leader was giving three final downbeats to the number. One… two…

BOINK!

He turned his head around. Lucian was leaving the dance floor, the arrow proudly in his hand. The irate society matron was rubbing her posterior.

THE WONDERFUL EDISON TIME MACHINE

Suddenly the sliding doors behind Jubee opened and several servants filed out with empty trays. A group of men could be seen talking in the library. Jubee nodded to Spiff, and the two boys quickly slipped inside.

CHAPTER THREE

THE MEETING IN THE LIBRARY

In the center of the room was an ornate table with a man seated beside it. Spaced around were a number of important-looking men in tuxedos and clown costumes. There was an air of urgency and cigar smoke. A man was speaking in a loud voice.

"We've borne enough insults from Detroit. It's time we made them understand we'll keep our current models with or without their approval."

"That's right," the crowd agreed. "There's no other way."

"Modernize Flint's auto plants to keep out foreign competition? We can't *afford* retooling. Let Detroit come out with newer models. We'll just *advertise* ours more."

There were several shouts of "Hear, hear." A fat man dressed as a caveman was seated next to the speaker. He smiled in an oily manner and continued to pet his toy leather dinosaur, which had "Ossified Motors" lettered on its side.

Jubee's eyes lit upon a pretty 16-year-old girl who was standing by the terrace doors and anxiously watching the proceedings. She was dressed as Little Bo Peep and carried a small wooden sheep with wheels.

Cried another man: "If Hoover keeps the tariff high, the public will *have* to buy our cars." And yet another said: "We build a hundred cars to every one of Europe's. And the Japanese? Sure, they make a car. My son has one." He placed a little wind-up car on the desk, where it buzzed forward a few inches and then flipped over. "That's all the competition we'll ever have from *them*," he said, and there was laughter.

The first man spoke again. "And what does the chairman of our cartel say?"

Jubee whispered quickly to his huddled friend. "That's my great-grandfather, George Willoughby. He owns the Wizzer Automobile Company."

Willoughby, a man of 49, paused a moment to reflect.

"Well, gentlemen, if Flint fights, I go with her. But like my father…" and here he indicated a stern-faced visage in a frame above the fireplace, "I hope the foreigners and the Detroit auto magnates will leave us here — in peace."

"But, George…" cried a man, while another said, "You can't mean that you want *competition*?"

"Most of the misery of the world has been caused by competition," replied George. "And when the competition was eliminated, no one ever knew what it was about."

At this there was general commotion and disagreement. Jubee noticed that the pretty girl had moved closer to the group.

There was another man in the room, standing aloofly by the fireplace. His name was Canaletto Rheostat, and he smoked his cigar quietly and looked at the others with disdain.

"Now, now, gentlemen," said the first man. "Mr. Rheostat's been abroad, I hear. Don't you agree with us, Mr. Rheostat?"

The man addressed took a step forward. "I think it's hard winning a trade war with words, gentlemen."

Bolling Baul, a man of temper, quickly took offense. "What do you mean, sir?"

"I mean, Mr. Baul, there's not a public institution for higher learning or technology in the whole of Flint. Not a single source for research into metallurgy, hydraulics, or even aerodynamics."

"What difference does that make, sir, to a gentleman?" demanded another man.

THE MEETING IN THE LIBRARY

"I'm afraid it's going to make a great deal of difference to a great many gentlemen, sir," replied Mr. Rheostat.

Said the hothead, "Are you hinting, Mr. Rheostat, that the foreign automobile companies can lick us?"

"No, I'm not hinting. I'm saying very plainly that the foreigners are as well equipped as we. They've got factories, shipyards, coal mines too, and a fleet to get their products to our shores. They also value education more, and work far harder than we do. They can bring a new car out in half the time we do, and their reliability approaches ours. They've become quite innovative, too, and when we let our tariff fall, as fall it must, all we'll have left is last year's models no one wants…and arrogance."

"That's treachery!" came a cry of protest.

"I'm sorry if the truth offends you," replied Rheostat.

Bolling Baul was close to crimson now. "Apologies aren't enough, sir. I hear you were turned out of the Edsel Ford School of Design, Mr. Canaletto Rheostat, and that you aren't received by any decent family in Saginaw — not even your own."

"I apologize again, sir, for all my shortcomings. I appear to be spoiling everybody's brandy and cigars, and dreams of victory in a trade war." With that, he turned and left the room. Spiff turned to Jubee and finding him still distracted by the girl, quickly took off after Rheostat.

"Well, that's just about what you could expect from someone like Canaletto Rheostat," said an angry onlooker. "He refused to debate," cried Bolling Baul.

Jubee's great-grandfather sought to calm him down. "Not quite that, Bolling," said Willoughby. "He just refused to take advantage of you."

"Take advantage of me?"

"Yes. He's memorized every fact ever printed in Forbes magazine. As he's proved a number of times against more intelligent heads than yours."

"I'll show him," said Bolling adamantly. "I read Barron's!" And he made to follow Mr. Rheostat.

THE WONDERFUL EDISON TIME MACHINE

"Now, now, please don't go," pleaded George. "You may be needed for more important fighting. A trade war may be imminent."

With that there came a rising commotion from outside the room, and the sound of running feet. A man burst through the doors and breathlessly cried out, "IT'S HERE!"

Consternation swept the room. "A trade war? A trade war? *WAR*?" One of the assemblage who had passed out drunk woke to proclaim his patriotism: "WAHR? Ah'm from the South. South Lyon."

"RUDY VALLEE AND HIS ORCHESTRA," shouted the intruder. To the spirited music of "Dixie," flappers rushed in shouting, "Rudy, Rudy." The men in the library hastily donned their party masks and clown hats, grabbed their plastic twirlers and paper whistles, and rushed out.

The 16-year-old girl stamped her feet in frustration as the men departed, then broke into tears. As Jubee watched, she threw down her wooden sheep and ran out onto the terrace. Only the fat man was left, patiently stroking his toy dinosaur.

* * * * *

In the meantime, Spiff had been running across the front lawn after the departing figure of Canaletto Rheostat, who was now approaching a waiting car. The man no sooner got in than a woman with a southern accent worriedly inquired, "How did it go?" "Frankly, my dear, they didn't give a damn," Rheostat replied as the car drove off.

Spiff, now balanced on the curb, was blocked from further pursuit by a line of cars preparing to enter the party. Turning, he was suddenly grabbed by an official-looking man who appeared as if from nowhere.

"Hey, black boy," the man demanded. "You see any liquor in there?"

Spiff was dazed. "Liquor? Where?"

"In the house. We know it's in there."

Spiff was still dazed. "I didn't see no liquor."

"Well, you probably wouldn't, you sawed-off sheik," the man said

THE MEETING IN THE LIBRARY

contemptuously, and pushed Spiff backward. The boy fell to the ground just as the man's two youthful assistants, both handling axes, slammed the door of a car they'd been searching and hurried over. They helped Spiff regain his feet.

"We've searched the cars for hours," the thin one said, "and ain't found nothing — just like all the other times."

"You chowderheads couldn't find piss in a chamber pot!" roared back their boss. "And how'd you get that shiner?"

"Some tall guy hit me with his megaphone," the fat one said remorsefully. His boss snarled in disgust.

The thin one held up a small white packet. "We found some dope on Billy Mundy," he said encouragingly.

"Yeah, and who used it?" said the man, examining the empty container and glaring at the pudgy one accusingly. "I've been a baaad, baaad boy," confessed the culprit who, with a series of whoops, took off on a short and dainty dance across the lawn. The boss collected them and knocked their heads together.

"Listen, dopes. We're *Prohibition* agents! It's *liquor* we're after. Right now hundreds of people up there are having a good time, and we can't do anything about it. Because we can't figure out how the booze is getting *in*. If we don't put some vim in the Volstead Act, we'll *all* be out of a job." With that, he kicked his two assistants, who saluted and ran away. Spiff was left to stagger off alone.

CHAPTER FOUR

THE GIRL IN THE GARDEN

Meanwhile, Jubee had retrieved the wooden sheep from among the waste of party favors and stepped out onto the terrace. He briefly looked around, then set off. His curiosity had been aroused, and he was searching for the girl. In the upper garden, he encountered only fleeting lovers along the paths and hedges. He descended a broad expanse of stairs and entered the more neglected lower garden. Here it was quieter, and the night seemed to close about him. Nothing stirred. Then he heard a sound. Advancing to some foliage, he parted a few branches and looked through. Beyond, beside a spraying fountain lit only by the moon, he saw the girl crying. She was the first real thing he'd seen in 1929, and with timidity he approached.

"Here," he said. "I found your sheep." He laid it down before her as she continued crying. "What are you crying for? Is it something the men said?"

"They're all so stupid," the girl replied, attempting to wipe her eyes. "That's what my brother says. And my father's the most stupid one of all."

"Why? What's he doing?"

"He isn't doing *anything*. That's why we're going to lose our automobile company, and the home that grandpa built, and...everything. It's all because of that stupid party."

"What party?" inquired Jubee.

"The one that never ends. The one you're here for."

"You mean that party never *ends*?"

BEYOND, BESIDE A SPRAYING FOUNTAIN LIT ONLY BY THE MOON,
JUBEE SAW THE GIRL CRYING.

THE GIRL IN THE GARDEN

"It just goes on, *forever*. If ten guests leave, another ten arrive. Twenty-four hours a day. It's taking all of father's money. It's like a family curse." She was so miserable she didn't see how alarmed Jubee had become.

"What family? Do you mean you *live here*?"

"Of course I live here. When I can find a bed that isn't filled. My family makes the Wizzer car."

Jubee began to feel faint. "The Wizzer car?" he gulped.

The girl looked at him, surprised. "Haven't you seen the ads of a man standing behind one of our cars and saying, 'I'm taking a Wizz'?"

"Then your father must be George Willoughby," said the boy.

"He is," replied the girl.

"Then you must be… *Mad Margaret!*"

"You bet I'm mad. And how did you know my name?"

Jubee stared at her, unbelievingly. "Why didn't you ever marry? Why did you turn out so weird? Why did you live alone in that house all your life?"

"What *are* you talking about?" said Margaret. "You're just as crazy as the rest of them. Go away!" And she went back to crying.

So Jubee left her to her solitude, and when he looked back, she seemed to merge with the night and the marble whiteness of the fountain.

*   *   *   *   *

It now came to Jubee how tired he was from the long journey they had made and the unexpected things he'd seen. No longer in his costume, he walked across the wide expanse of lawn and headed toward the out-building where they had arrived. The party had thinned somewhat. From the house, Rudy Vallee could be heard crooning "My Time is Your Time." Dud chanced by, and they headed in the same direction.

"What's that you're eating?" Jubee inquired.

"It's called a Tin Roof," Dud replied. "Hot chocolate over peanuts and ice cream. There's a whole soda fountain in the basement. And they've got Jujubes…in silver bowls. You didn't need to bring your own. Here, try some."

The Wonderful Edison Time Machine

Jubee took a handful. "Have you seen Spiff and Lucifer?"

"They've already turned in." He looked at Jubee. "You find out anything?"

"Only that we lost our automobile company because of this stupid party."

"Yeah, I've heard it never stops. They sure know how to live in 1929," said Dud, and his voice receded as they continued on.

When they reached their room, the light revealed Spiff and Lucian in sleeping bags. Dud indicated the younger lad and observed, "He's like an angel when he's sleeping." Jubee lifted the sleeping bag and dumped his brother out. "You forget that Lucifer was a *fallen angel*," he explained. There came a muffled "God damn it" as Lucian groggily felt his way to an adjoining couch. Dud and Jubee then settled in.

"So what's on for tomorrow?" Dud inquired.

"We're going to the bank," said Jubee.

"How much money you plan on getting?"

"Three hundred million dollars."

Spiff and Lucian rose up. "THREE HUNDRED MILLION DOLLARS?"

Dud rolled over and closed his eyes.

"Don't ask for it in ones."

CHAPTER FIVE

A VISIT TO THE BANK

As dawns do come, it came, and the streets of the slumbering city of Flint were soon awash in golden streaks of sunshine. But few people were about in the early morning hour, and fewer still to see three exceedingly odd hats bobbing up and down behind a fence. A moment later a dilapidated horse-drawn wagon came into view, slowly winding its way down a cobbled street to an Oriental-sounding "The Japanese Sandman." Loosely nailed to its side was a hand-painted sign: "Krockashita and Sons, Secondhand Junk."

Three men sat atop the wagon. One was Osocka, the grandfather, who wore a conical hat and had a long white beard. Another was Gosoaka, his son, who wore a peasant's hat. The last was Unseemly, *his* son, barely out of his teens. He sported a military cap. They all looked like fugitives from a rice paddy and were singing "The Japanese Sandman" in reedy voices:

"Here's the Japanese Junk Men
Getting up with the dew.
Just some old second-hand men,
And your trash they'll go through."

They stopped by a row of trash cans. Bowing and scraping to one another they approached the cans and began to rummage through them. Soon they uncovered some jumbled blueprints and calculating tapes and removed them as Gosoaka continued the song.

THE WONDERFUL EDISON TIME MACHINE

"They're just looking for discards,
And some prints that are blue.
Plus your old calculations
They can figure anew."

Osocka held aside a week-old fish, while Unseemly put in his two yens' worth.

"Please don't wake from your slumber,
Please don't question your fate.
When the dawn brings you wisdom,
You will find it's too late."

A Visit to the Bank

The three men then regained the wagon with their findings and departed down the street, again singing in unison:

"Here's the Japanese Junk Men
Getting up with the dew.
Just some old second-hand men..."

A shaft of morning sunlight struck Dud asleep in his bed. He opened his eyes, then struggled out of his sleeping bag. He grabbed his shirt and crossed over to the window. In the distance the Japanese junkmen could still be heard. He looked over at Jubee, who was already dressed and was copying figures from his notebook. The door opened and Spiff came in, laden with breakfast dishes.

"The party's still going on," he said. "They're even serving breakfast."

He put the dishes down, including a tray of doughnuts. Lucian was still asleep, but his arm moved independently and took a doughnut. Spiff told Dud there was a head just down the hall, then moved to where Jubee was.

"Is it safe to leave the Time Machine alone?" he worried. "It's our only means of getting back. Perhaps one of us should guard it."

"Guard something we *know* will still be here in 1991?" scoffed Jubee. "Because that's when we found it and used it. No harm can come to it 'til then."

Spiff was not convinced. "What if the Time Machine in 1991 is destroyed? Then it can't call us back. We're going to be here half a year."

"I've thought of that," his friend replied. "So I programmed the machine to recall us from November 2, 1929, just *one minute* after we left. Not much can happen in one minute."

"You forget Mad Margaret was breaking down the door. What if she wrecks the Time Machine?"

"She won't," said Jubee. "Not if we're successful here. Let's go!"

A short time later the boys were walking on North Saginaw. The day was beautiful, and the city throbbed with hope and exhilaration. Passersby were clean and neat no matter what their station, and the stores were open and inviting, with proprietors out front to welcome customers inside. The air was cool and fresh, and the world seemed young, and everyone to have a purpose.

Spiff did not notice that their collegiate costumes were causing stares, as his mind was elsewhere.

"You must be delirious," he remonstrated Jubee. "The whole city of Flint isn't worth even thirty million dollars. Someone should take your temperature."

His friend was looking at a slip of paper. "I'll take yours with a telephone pole if you don't shut up."

They passed a Good Humor man, and Lucian felt an immediate need for nutrients. He ran to the others and held out some change.

"Jubee, can I buy an ice cream bar?"

Absently, his brother paused. "No, you can't buy a...you mean you've got *money*?" He grabbed the coins and examined one. "Oh, fine! 1980 money in 1929, plus you're wearing *Nike shoes!*"

He and Dud held the boy upside down and shook out everything, including a yo-yo, a decoder badge and six more coins. They then pulled off his shoes and continued on, leaving a woozy Lucian to recover.

Spiff strove to keep up. "So you think you can walk into any bank in Flint and walk out with a million dollars?"

Jubee stopped, looked at his slip, then up at the massive portals of the FLINT INDUSTRIAL TRUST. "Not just *any* bank," he said. "*This* bank!"

Gingerly the boys walked through its columned entrance. Jubee and Dud headed toward a marble balustrade, while the other two remained behind. There was a desk with a flapper secretary behind the partition. She was chewing gum and adjusting her silk stockings.

Jubee removed his hat and said subserviently, "I'd like to see Mr. Huron Greenwich."

"He isn't in," the secretary said.

A Visit to the Bank

"Then Mr. Morrow C. Cardington."

"You got a name?" she asked.

"Tell him 'Sonny Boy' is here."

The secretary shrugged and pressed a button. A low gate opened and she indicated a direction, then spoke into a speaker box. Jubee departed toward a large desk, while Dud remained to admire the girl's legs. That, plus the rest of her, he had never seen anything like, before.

Spiff stood by the bank's entrance, with Lucian in tow. He noted the black doorman who, with obsequious bows, ushered in the customers, all of whom were white. He surveyed the bank. Not a black in sight. No, there was one: a janitor, who was emerging from a door with mop and bucket.

Mr. Cardington proved to be an important-looking man seated at his desk. It held a container of cigars and a bronze desk calendar which read "Monday - May 6, 1929."

"Mr. Cardington?" said Jubee.

"Yes, 'Sonny Boy,' I believe. What can I do for you?"

Jubee gave him his most ingratiating smile. "I go to Central High School over on Crapo Street, and our teacher is having us study the stock market."

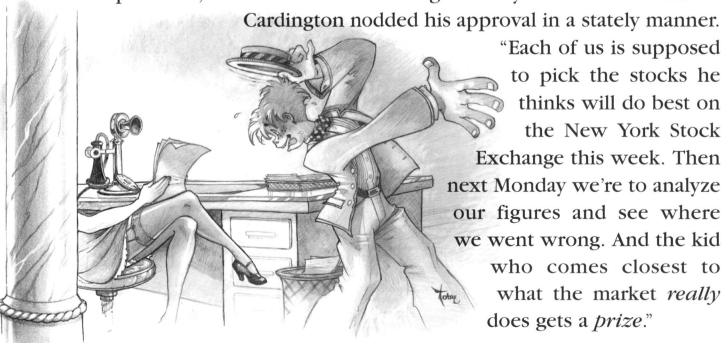

Cardington nodded his approval in a stately manner. "Each of us is supposed to pick the stocks he thinks will do best on the New York Stock Exchange this week. Then next Monday we're to analyze our figures and see where we went wrong. And the kid who comes closest to what the market *really* does gets a *prize*."

"What's the prize?" asked Cardington.

"A weekend on Zug Island."

"You'd be better off to lose. Besides, I don't know anything about the market."

"You don't have to," Jubee said. "We're just supposed to *talk* to an adult. I've already picked my stocks. See?"

Jubee handed him a list. "For each day I've listed the stocks I think will go up most, and the figure they will close at. I've even predicted each day's sales for the entire week."

Cardington quickly scanned the list. "You're very thorough. But really, Wright Aeronautical up nine points? More likely it will dive. We got out of *that* dog six weeks ago."

"Wait and see," the boy replied. "Just check each day how close I've come and put the real figures beside mine. Then after the market closes Saturday, we can go over my mistakes. On Monday I'll be able to tell my teacher the *best banker* in Michigan gave me advice."

Cardington was hooked. "Well, I'll do it if it helps you." He pocketed the list.

"There's just *one* thing," added Jubee, his eyes sweeping the room suspiciously. "All this is *super secret*. Don't show my list to *anyone*. Scout's honor?"

"Scout's honor!" chucked Mr. Cardington.

"Gee, thanks!" said Jubee as he turned to leave. "See you this Saturday." He walked back across the carpet and found Dud trying to impress the secretary.

"You'll be in diamonds, baby," he solemnly intoned. She gave him the look of death.

"C'mon," said Jubee, taking his crestfallen friend's arm. "The trap is set." They advanced to where the other two were waiting.

"I ordered our new Chrysler in blue," said Spiff sarcastically. "Hope that's okay."

"Just so it can get us to the Rolls-Royce agency. But the money won't start coming in for several weeks. I told you that."

Dud observed, "What do we do until then? Starve?"

"With that free lunch at our house? And we've got Spiff's gold coin to live on for awhile."

"Just so we replace it with another," admonished Spiff. "My mom's a hawk. It's all we've left of great-grand daddy Birdsong, except for his prison papers."

They exited past the bowing doorman and were immediately confronted by a passing truant officer holding a pole and net. "Hey! Why aren't you kids in school?" he barked.

"School?" said Dud bleakly.

Jubee made a quick aside. "In the 1920s kids were expected to be in school. It's one of the things that made it so quaint."

"Well, I didn't come this far to go to school," groused Dud.

The truant officer loomed threateningly. "You'd better make it good."

"We go to a private school," said Jubee, suddenly inspired.

"Yeah? What one?"

"Jockmore."

"Never heard of it."

"You never heard of the Jockmore Jocks?" Jubee was incredulous.

Dud chipped in. "Just last week they beat the crapo out of Central."

"Well, I don't know," growled the officer.

Spiff spied a waiting town car with a sleeping chauffeur and announced, "The Jockmore Jalopy awaits!" He ran over and opened its rear door. The boys filed past the perplexed officer in injured dignity and entered the car. Lucian was last and gave the man the finger. Spiff pulled him inside, then stuck his head out the window. "Home, James," he instructed the startled chauffeur, who proceeded to drive the car away just as a well-dressed woman approached, followed by a sales clerk carrying packages. She looked at her departing car in disbelief.

*　*　*　*

Afternoon found them in "The Toggery – Duds for the Discriminating."

THE WONDERFUL EDISON TIME MACHINE

The boys were preening happily in their new clothes, while Spiff reluctantly paid for them with his gold coin.

Evening found them crossing over to the party. They crammed huge sandwiches in their mouths and watched jazz musicians play. Margaret saw and snubbed them. They made a sundae in the basement big enough to ski on, and when they retired to their secret room they rubbed their stomachs in blissful satisfaction.

*   *   *   *   *

The next morning Cardington was having breakfast. A picture of importance, the banker had just finished the newspaper. He remembered his promise to Jubee and removed the list of stock quotations from his vest. He chuckled to himself and reopened the paper to the financial section. He took a pencil and looked at the first stock and noted its closing figure beside the boy's: "Am Bank Note +3 = 129." He wrote down 129. Jubee's figure was the same. The banker smiled and shrugged.

"Bloomingdale Bros. +3 = 58." He hesitated, then wrote down 58. Jubee's figure was the same. The banker now looked puzzled.

"By-Products Coke +5 = 130." He wrote down 130. The banker now was angry. He grabbed the paper and wrote down figures furiously.

Jubee's Figures	Newspaper's Figures
Eaton Axle +3 = **68**	EA-**68**
Fox Film +4 = **96**	FF-**96**
Indian Motorcycle +3 = **20**	IM-**20**
Inter. Tel & Tel +6 = **270**	ITT-**270**
Orpheum Circ. +4 = **85**	OC-**85**
Phoenix Hosiery +3 = **31**	PH-**31**
Pitts & West. Va. +4 = **135**	P&W-**135**
United Air & Trans +7 = **155**	UAT-**155**
West. Maryland +4 = **46**	WM-**46**

THE BOYS PREENED HAPPILY IN THEIR NEW TOGS.

A Visit to the Bank

The final stock was Wright Aeronautical, the one he said would dive. It had advanced to 147. The banker's hand shook as he penciled in the same amount. And now came "Total sales: 3,813,080." With dread, he looked at Jubee's figure.

Cardington fell back.

"HOLY MOTHER OF GOD!" he said.

CHAPTER SIX

THE HARBOR CLUB

Jubee's plan required several days to work. So the next morning they got up late. Not having any money, they partook of breakfast by the pool, then decided to stick around the house. No one ever questioned them, and by late afternoon the party was again like several New Year's Eves rolled into one. The two Prohibition agents were again searching cars and catering trucks for liquor, to the increasing frustration of their boss. Margaret saw a group of girls about to pick up Jubee, so she shyly smiled at him.

Things for Cardington, however, were anything but normal. Each day he wrote down stock figures and compared them to Jubee's. Each day Jubee's were the same. It was fantastic; it couldn't happen; it had to be a trick. May 8, May 9, May 10. His tie was now undone, his shirt open, his eyes were glazed from sleepless nights, and he drank like Prohibition never happened.

Each night Jubee also stayed up late. He was making out a new stock list, one to give to Cardington. Dud spent his time gazing at the moon, while Spiff and Lucian were long asleep.

* * * * *

Saturday found Jubee again before the banker's desk. The calendar read May 11. Cardington looked up to see the young boy staring at him.

"Sonny Boy," said Cardington weakly.

Jubee reached for a cigar. "I told you I'd be back."

The banker stopped him with his hand. "How did you do that?" he said.

"My stock market list? That doesn't matter. What does matter is I can do it again."

"Again?" gasped Cardington.

"Here's my list for next week. We can cut the crap about these being *predictions*. They're *facts*. Right now only *two* people in the entire world know what the New York Stock Exchange will do next week, and you're *one* of them."

"What do you want me to do?" asked Cardington.

"Nothing. Except show this list to Greenwich and Worthington. Swear them to secrecy. Then meet me outside the bank next Saturday at five. I'll have a proposition for you, one I'd like to discuss over dinner. Some place private, where you won't be recognized."

"A proposition? What's it about?"

"It's about thirty million dollars, and keeping you guys out of *jail!*" With that, Jubee spun around and walked away. Cardington was left staring into space.

Dud was standing by the secretary. She was examining his latest offering, a cheap ring in an even cheaper box. "Looks like you went the limit at Woolworth's," she yawned, and dropped it in the wastebasket. Dud was again crestfallen, and he followed Jubee dejectedly to where the others were waiting, and they exited.

Outside, the truant officer was passing by. "So, it's you wise guys again," he snarled.

"You can't bother us," Dud retorted. "It's *Saturday*."

"Oh, yeah? I was out Wednesday, so I'm making up for it. And don't give me any of that crap about 'Jockmore.' There ain't no such school in Genesee County."

"That's because it's *strapped* for cash," cried Jubee, and the boys collapsed together in laughter.

"Get it?" said Dud. "Jock, strap, *strapped* for cash! Ha, ha, ha, ha, ha."

THE WONDERFUL EDISON TIME MACHINE

"Levity is lost on him," said Spiff. "'The Fight Song.'" Instantly the three of them assumed cheerleader positions while Lucian darted behind the officer and got down.

"Jockmore, Jockmore,
From Eau Clair to Des Moines.
When no one's looking, we get cooking,
And HIT 'EM IN THE GROIN."

They pushed the man over and took off running.

*   *   *   *   *

Cardington was still staring into space when his phone rang. It was Worthington.

"Greenwich is cracking. I don't know if he'll go along. We're down another quarter mil. There's no way we can dig out. It'd take a *miracle*."

"Pay it," replied Cardington. "Juggle the books any way you can. Then stop by my desk. I think the miracle just happened."

*   *   *   *   *

The next few days went swiftly. The junkmen continued their appointed rounds, and one lunchtime Unseemly ate rice cakes and read *Popular Mechanics* upside down while his partners removed old blueprints from a Hoover Vacuum Company bin. Margaret showed the kids how to Charleston. Cardington, Worthington and Greenwich spent their time perusing Jubee's second list of stocks and making computations. Friday found the boys retiring early to their secret room. Jubee was making a new stock list for his next day's meeting with the bankers. Spiff and Lucian were playing Chinese Checkers, and Dud was reading a book by Elinor Glyn.

"Do you think I have 'It?'" he suddenly inquired.

"Herpes or crabs?" replied his friends.

*   *   *   *   *

For all their fun and nonchalant acceptance of the past, the world of 1929 was beginning to get to the boys. Things that *looked* familiar really weren't. It was like what the "Retard of Avon" (Dud's irreverent name for Shakespeare) had said about things undergoing a sea change.

For one thing, there were telephones, but if you talked on them, *real people* answered, and you could not dial Poland on your own. And there were radios, but they looked like churches, and nobody bared their sex life on them. There were movies, but you had to see them in a theater, and your choice was limited to one. There were airplanes, but they carried at most ten passengers and bounced aloft on non-retractable landing gear.

One rarely saw a truck outside the city. But there were trains, and they were everywhere, hissing and groaning and releasing plumes of steam, binding the nation together on endless rails of steel. Harbingers of prosperity, they carried the bulk of the country's commerce, as well as throngs of passengers who were disgorged on vast concourses that led into terminals as big as temples in a Roman forum.

There were cars, and even traffic jams, but these cars were not smarter than their owners, and they seemed fun to drive. They required your full attention just to keep them moving, so you could not do a hundred other things while at the wheel. Drivers were not hermetically sealed within an antiseptic world of their own, and best of all, there were no parking meters. Plus everyone wore hats.

But perhaps the strangest was the lack of any sense of danger on the streets of Flint. The boys did not have to walk defensively, or think defensively, or wonder if the next person they encountered was looking for the O.K. Corral. Eyes willingly met eyes, and no one seemed to claim a personal space inviolate to others. Homes were not fortresses and windows were not barred, and if a house was bothered to be locked, a skeleton key would usually open it.

Somehow the city seemed *proud* of its inhabitants, or at least *tolerant* of them, and in subtle ways it made known what was *expected* of them, rather than what was *demanded*. Increasingly the boys wondered how *their* world had lost these things. But Spiff was beginning to see there was a darker side, and even Dud and Jubee were vaguely apprehensive, as if caught in a story by Ray Bradbury. At times they felt like fish in a fish bowl, being watched by an unseen cat.

*　*　*　*　*

Saturday afternoon found all four of them lolling near the entrance to the bank. The last few customers left, then the door was locked and the blind lowered. The kids looked at each other, perplexed. There then came a loud "Psst." Cardington was beckoning to them from a nearby alley. They ran to him immediately. Down the alley by the bank's side entrance was an ancient taxi cab, its sides painted with the words "The Checkered Career Cab Co." Its driver was a graying black man who wore a frayed chauffeur's coat and sat exposed to the elements. Greenwich and Worthington were just slipping inside. Spiff and Lucian jumped in the front seat while the other two boys sat on jump seats in the back. As Greenwich pulled down the window shades, Cardington picked up the speaking tube.

"Take us to the Harbor Club," he commanded.

"*The Harbor Club*?"

"And don't take Saginaw. Take back streets."

"That's Slugsy's place," the driver protested. "Ah wondered why you didn't call a respectable cab company. But Ah can't take *kids* there."

Cardington was adamant. "Do you want the bank to call your loan?"

"No, Sah. The Flint Industrial Trust has been mighty good to me. Only thirty percent interest."

"The Mafia charges thirty-five," said the banker. "So get this tub moving."

"Yes, Sah," the driver said, resigned.

*　*　*　*　*

The Harbor Club was a dreary-looking clapboard building out by Devil's Lake. In better days it had been a cannery. Large cut-out letters on the roof announced its name. Wolves howled in the distance.

The Harbor Club

Inside, the group was escorted to a secluded wooden booth. The four boys sat on one side, the bankers on the other. All appeared nervous and self-conscious. A tattooed waiter wearing a soiled apron entered through the beaded curtain. He distributed some menus, then saw the kids.

"Hey, wot's dis? We can't have no kids here, 'lessen they're part of the act."

"We come on right after Lola and the donkey," deadpanned Spiff.

"Gee! Is Lola back?"

The waiter disappeared and they all began studying the menus. Suddenly a shapely white female leg came through the beads, bejeweled hands caressing it and dangling a garter. No one paid any attention, and it was withdrawn. Then shapely yellow and black legs appeared. Again there was no reaction, and they were withdrawn. Finally a muscular *man's* leg was presented, but it too was ignored.

Then an Asian hand in a gorgeous silk sleeve presented a three-pronged pipe of opium. Worthington absently accepted it and passed it down the line. None partook of it until it reached Lucian. The lad made to take a satisfying gulp, but Dud snatched it away from him and passed it on to Jubee, who passed it on to Spiff, who returned it to the hand. They continued studying their menus.

A whip was presented through the curtains, then a chain and paddle. Two hands shuffling a deck of cards were next, then dice. Finally, in desperation, a sign appeared: "Tennis, anyone?" There were no takers and it too was withdrawn.

Lucian saw Greenwich adjusting his pince-nez with a small screwdriver. The lad picked it up and examined the table-model one-armed bandit by his side at the end of the booth. He began to tinker with it just as the waiter reappeared to take their order.

With that accomplished, Jubee began officiating. "Let's get down to business. I know you guys are stealing money from your bank to speculate in the stock market. You're down at least a million dollars, and there's no way you can make it up. When the crash comes you'll lose everything and all be sent to prison. It'll be in all the history books."

Worthington turned to Cardington. "I told you things looked gray."

"Prison! Our friends may forsake us," said Greenwich.

"No more singing in the church choir," said Worthington, griefstricken.

Cardington waved them quiet. "You say a crash is coming?"

"The biggest financial crash in U.S. history is just around the corner. It'll be followed by a depression that will last ten years."

"Can you pull us through?" pleaded Worthington.

"Yes," said Jubee. "Because you've got access to unlimited money, and *I* know which stocks to buy. Together we can turn your gray skies into *blue*. All you have to do is follow me." He unfolded a paper.

"Here's what the market's going to do next week. Look at the top three stocks I've listed. They alone, if you buy on margin, will net you over half a million dollars. Buy them all and next Saturday we'll be millionaires."

There was consternation among the bankers.

"In two months you'll make thirty million dollars and never have to go to jail. It's a plan that's made in heaven. What do you say?"

The bankers hurriedly conferred. As they broke, a gypsy violinist appeared through the curtain and began playing "Sonny Boy," accompanied by others outside. Worthington dolefully began to sing the song. "When there are gray skies, we don't mind the gray skies…"

Cardington then joined in: "You'll paint them blue, Sonny Boy."

"Friends may forsake us, let them all forsake us," included Greenwich, and then they all added in together: "You'll pull us through, Sonny Boy."

"You're sent from heaven, and we know you were." Cardington wiped away a tear. "You've made a heaven for us right here on earth." Worthington blew his nose.

Greenwich had to strain to reach a high note. "But if the angels grow lonely, take you 'cause they're lonely…"

They all three finished, more or less together: "We'll follow you, Sonny Boy."

The violinist left and all six participants jubilantly shook hands, and then looked hungrily as the waiter entered with a succulent feast of Chinese dishes.

Lucian, meanwhile, was deep in the innards of the slot machine. A bell rang and a single cherry appeared, then disappeared. "Looks like you lost your cherry," commented Dud. Lucian glared at him and returned to work. He removed a screw and the machine short-circuited. The bell rang and four cherries appeared, then again and again. The machine was going berserk. Then to a foghorn "B.O.," the machine stopped. Lucian looked at it expectantly. A single slug rolled out. The boy held it up in disgust.

"Looks like you struck out," laughed Dud.

Lucian angrily punched the machine. Immediately a thousand nickels spurted out and overflowed the food.

CHAPTER SEVEN

WAITING FOR WEALTH

The next several weeks passed in quick succession. Margaret introduced Jubee to her mother and father, who were dressed as the Roman deities Juno and Jupiter. The boy could hardly keep his face straight. Later he met her brother, David, who seemed a fine young man, and her sister, Imogene, whom Jubee recognized as the infatuated girl he saw feeding grapes to an anemic British lord the first night he arrived.

The bankers spent their time around a glass-topped stock ticker, which chattered out an endless tape they viewed with increasing fascination. They transferred the numbers to an adding machine and rubbed their chins in wonder at the growing wealth. Money rained down on them as if from an awesome height.

Jubee spent more time with Margaret. One evening they were sitting by the pool when there came a sudden "twang." The boy jumped, then pulled a rubber arrow from his back. He looked around for the perpetrator, but did not see his little brother, dressed as Cupid, posing atop a nearby fountain. He noted the arrow's series of red hearts and showed it to Margaret. She laughed, and they moved closer together.

* * * * *

Friday, May 24, found Jubee again at the bank. Cardington was beaming over Jubee's latest list, and the boy pocketed some money. He also took a cigar.

"That's another two hundred dollars on account," he said. "We're three

LUCIAN SAW THE OLDER BOYS BEING CHASED BY THE TRUANT OFFICER
AND IMMEDIATELY BEGAN CRANKING THE CAR.

million dollars ahead now, so Greenwich can quit having cooties. Next Friday the three million will be *thirty*. In seven more days we can *all* begin to *live*." He then crossed to the gate where Dud was panting over the secretary. This time she held a cheap tiara.

"Macy's Bargain Basement," she observed. "You're coming up in the world." She discarded it with scorn. An angry Dud joined Jubee, and the exit door was opened for them. Cautiously they stepped outside.

A few yards away the truant officer spotted them. The boys took off. Down the street Spiff was waiting in the driver's seat of an ancient Chevrolet. It had a raccoon tail and sported slogans such as "Oh you kid," "The Jockmore Jalopy" and "It's Jockmore Two by One." Lucian, wearing an old-fashioned duster coat and goggles, was waiting by the car. He saw the older boys being chased and immediately began cranking the motor while Spiff waved frantically at him.

The truant officer was gaining on them, so Dud toppled a garbage can, which the man fell over. They dove into the car just as Spiff and Lucian got it started. Lucian was pulled aboard at the last moment, and the car roared away just as the truant officer arrived, his face strewn with garbage.

* * * * *

Cardington's desk calendar showed May 27, 28, 29 and 30. Two of the bankers were now using *five* adding machines, while the third spoke on several phones at once. Their broker, on the other end, shouted frantically as he examined a stream of market tape. Behind him, graphs on the wall had lines going only up, up, up. Money swirled down in an increasing blizzard, and an armored car pulled up before the bank.

* * * * *

Oblivious to the finer facets of finance, Jubee and Margaret took a late night stroll one evening beside Long Lake behind the mansion. They passed the house next door. A man in a tuxedo was standing on a terrace looking out across the water. Jubee looked back at him.

THE WONDERFUL EDISON TIME MACHINE

"That's our neighbor, Mr. Gatsby," Margaret explained. "He's a little strange." Then, in a more serious vein, she asked, "Why are you always eating Jujubes?"

"'Cause I like 'em," Jubee replied.

"That's how you got your name, isn't it?"

"Yep!" said Jubee, handing her the box. "Want some?"

"They stick to my teeth. I've never seen this kind of box before...Seventy-five cents FOR A NICKEL BOX OF CANDY?"

Jubee retrieved the candy in alarm. "They're a special kind," he hastily explained. "Made just for me in Cuba. They roll them there by hand."

"At that price, the box should be solid gold," his girlfriend protested.

The two young people headed from the beach, and did not see the two dark figures in the nearby brush. One had lifted a machine gun, but the other one cautioned him to pause. The teenagers veered away, and the gun was lowered.

On the following day, *three* armored cars with police escorts pulled up outside the bank. They began unloading bags of money and securities. Cardington, stacks of new boxes of cash beside him, opened the bank vault. To his dismay, it was completely filled, and the money still rained down. But it meant they all were *rich*.

*   *   *   *   *

Friday, May 31, 1929. The four boys were in happy spirits as they approached the bank. This was the payoff day. A man in a heavy coat with a hat pulled over his eyes was lounging near the entrance. At the last moment he lit a cigarette and hurried off. Behind him was a sign: "Bank Remodeling — Please Use Side Entrance."

The boys saw it and turned into the alley. Ahead of them was a curtained structure with a notice and a few steps leading up. They mounted them and went inside. Immediately the man reappeared and slid a barred gate shut. The curtain parted and the truant officer's cage and a Flint School District sign were revealed. The kids rushed to the bars. They had been captured.

CHAPTER EIGHT

THE ORPHANS OF OPIUM ALLEY

Within a matter of hours the older boys found themselves in a large, dingy hall with barred windows. They wore drab uniforms and their arms were loaded with cheap bedding. In the distance a girl was singing, "The sun'll come out tomorrow."

"You *had* to tell them we were orphans," Spiff said accusingly.

"What else could I say?" retorted Jubee. "I couldn't tell them where we *really* live. We'll get out of here."

Dud was resigned. "Just as we were coming into dough."

They began making their beds. The girl, still bellowing the song, appeared in the background. She was accompanied by a large, bushy-tailed dog and was skipping rope. She stopped, momentarily.

"Hi! I'm Little Orphan Fanny."

The boys ignored her and continued working. She skipped away, only to immediately reappear doing circles on roller skates.

"My dog's name is 'Dandy.' You can't pet him."

The boys took no notice and she skated off, only to return doing an energetic side-step in which she brought her knees together and crossed her hands between them. Her eyes were rolled up.

"Look, no eyes!" she said.

Failing to impress them, she wandered off, continuing to sing her song, as the boys sat down to ponder their fate.

THE WONDERFUL EDISON TIME MACHINE

* * * * *

Hours later the kids were still in the same position. Some of the other beds now contained children. In the distance, Fanny was still singing the same song.

"Doesn't she *ever* shut up?" said Jubee.

At that moment a plain but sweet orphan entered the scene. She had a clipboard and was doing bed check.

"Hi! I'm Rosemary. You're new here, aren't you? I haven't seen *you* before."

"Well, take a good look, sister," said Jubee grimly. "We're breaking out of here tonight."

"Oh, you can't," the girl replied. "The walls are too high. I've been here *ten years*."

"Can't you get adopted?" Dud asked.

"Nobody wants me." She then saw Jubee mouthing Jujubes. "Oh, *candy!* We get candy here at Christmas."

Jubee poured her some. "Do you know where my little brother is?"

"They put *him* in solitary."

"Well, can you get me to him?"

"Miss Hanniberry said she threw away the key." The girl looked concerned.

"Well," said Jubee, "can you get me to a telephone?" He turned to the others. "Cardington will get us out of this."

THE ORPHANS OF OPIUM ALLEY

"There's one in the downstairs hallway. I can leave the door open for you. But it's a pay phone. You'll need a nickel."

"Can you lend me one?" asked Jubee. "I'll pay you back."

"I had a nickel at Christmas," said Rosemary.

"Maybe we can break into the coin box. Leave the door open for us. We won't forget you, I promise."

The girl left, and Dud and Jubee began rearranging their beds as if someone was sleeping in them.

"C'mon, Spiff," said Jubee. "We're getting out of here."

"What? *And miss Christmas*?"

The others grabbed him and they left.

* * * * *

Gingerly, the boys snuck down the stairs. It was quiet as a tomb, and the walls were bilious. They came upon a cheerless table covered with some oilcloth and containing dog-eared magazines most news stands would not carry. Beyond it was the telephone and Little Orphan Fanny, who was engaged in earnest conversation. She was smoking a cigarette and wearing a bathrobe and shower cap. Beside her was her wig, a scrubbing brush and a small suitcase.

"Listen, Hot Lead," she was saying. "I'm almost forty now and this is the *last time* I'm playing the part of a vacant-eyed eight-year-old loudmouth so *you* can extort money from Daddy Morebucks.

"I've been kidnapped by pirates, fricasseed by cannibals, sold to white slavers, and gone stir-crazy in orphanages on *five continents*, all so you could tell that bald-headed old fart where I was and *get paid* for it. It's time we settled down. We've both got dough, and you won't be the first pimp ever to get married." She paused.

"Yes, I got rid of the damn dog. I traded him to Miss Hanniberry for a highball. You just make sure Punjoke is here in one hour. And tell that Hindu fakir not to get *fresh*. I'll wait by the second-floor window. Tomorrow I'll give

THE WONDERFUL EDISON TIME MACHINE

Morebucks the slip and meet you at the hotel."

With that she hung up and went through swinging doors into the kitchen. The kids peered through, then followed her. They passed a wooden table with a meat grinder from which a bushy tail stuck out. Beside it was a dog collar and a long, fat stream of sausages. The boys continued on into another hallway and a nearby lavatory. There came the sound of water splashing, and when they cautiously inched open the door, Fanny was behind a curtain singing lustily:

"The sun'll come out tomorrow; bet your bottom dollar that tomorrow, there'll be sun…"

They spied her clothes and suitcase by a makeup table. The boys grabbed them, and as they left Dud removed the key from inside the door and locked it from the outside.

Minutes later Spiff was being made up as Little Orphan Fanny. He had on her dress, her shoes, her wig, and was holding her purse. Jubee professionally applied some last-minute lipstick and face powder as Dud watched by the window.

"No good will come of this," said Spiff.

"Quit griping," Jubee told him. "You're the closest one in size."

THE ORPHANS OF OPIUM ALLEY

Dud then froze them all. "Someone's coming."

Down on a street of shadowed warehouses, a large dark form was moving. It wore a turban, carried a basket, and made not the slightest sound. As the boys watched breathlessly from above, the figure put the basket down, set its lid aside, and began to play a flute. Immediately two ropes appeared, appraised the situation, and insidiously wound their way toward the window.

The kids were frightened as the ropes weaved back and forth outside the window and softly hissed like cobras. Then the music ended and the ropes froze into steps. Bravely, and with a minimal amount of goosing, Spiff moved out, then carefully romped down them. He skipped over to a nearby street sign that said "Opium Alley" and stood under it, looking all the world like a hooker.

Then Jubee started down, Dud holding him. Suddenly the stairs went slack, and Jubee was left dangling. Dud managed to pull him back inside, and they both called down in falsetto voices.

"Yoo-hoo, dearie," Jubee cried. "You forgot you're on the pill." He rattled his box of Jujubes.

Dud waved Spiff's underwear. "And your undies. Don't be indecent."

Spiff as Fanny gestured helplessly to Punjoke, and the rope ladder reappeared. The boys climbed down and ran over to their friend just as a sinister black limousine glided up. It was driven by a spectral entity known as "The Viper." The kids jumped in and the car moved off.

The boys seemed lost in the vastness of the car. Polished wood gleamed dully in the muted light, and there were robes and pillows of the richest fabrics on every side. An inlaid cabinet filled with crystal goblets lay in front of them, and a duplicate panel of dashboard instruments calibrated engine functions the boys would never have thought possible. Beyond, and through a heavy glass partition, could be seen the rigid forms of their two liberators. The car purred like a well-trained beast and effortlessly transported them through the lonely outer streets of the sleeping city, where hardly a light appeared among the houses that they passed.

The Wonderful Edison Time Machine

Eventually the car pulled up before a swank apartment house, and Punjoke and The Viper hauled an unwilling Spiff up its steps. Dud and Jubee were left outside. A light went on in a first-floor window.

"I wonder how long it will take Daddy Morebucks to find out," said Jubee apprehensively.

From the house came a loud:

"AARRGGUGH!"

"Not very long, I'd say," said Dud, and they both took off.

CHAPTER NINE

FALCONS AND FETISHES

It was noon, the next day. The three boys were in the swank apartment, seated in armchairs by an end table that held the statue of a black bird. Daddy Morebucks sat across from them, a balding authoritative man of immense wealth. Behind him The Viper was skillfully throwing knives, while Punjoke softly fluted his ropes.

Morebucks was in a reflective mood. "I've searched all over the world for her."

"The Maltese Falcon?" Dud guessed.

"No. My rosy-cheeked Fanny." He picked up a long folded list. "Just in the last three years I've rescued her from Aachen, Addis Ababa, Adelaide, Agra, Ankara, Ann Arbor…"

Jubee broke in. "You'll never find her this time without *my* help. And I'm not turning her over until I'm *good* and *ready*." A knife then split the chair just inches from his face.

"I'm *ready*," he confessed.

The boy removed the knife and used it to cut a cigar, while Punjoke's ropes intertwined into a hangman's noose. Dud was examining the Maltese Falcon.

"What do you propose?" said Morebucks. He formed his fingers into a bridge.

"A fair exchange," said Jubee. Dud was scraping the Maltese Falcon with an ashtray. "I want you to adopt my little brother for five months so he can get out of the orphanage. In other words, his *ass* for your Fanny."

THE WONDERFUL EDISON TIME MACHINE

"Not a chance," waved Morebucks. "I find little boys disgusting. Let's talk *money*." Dud was bashing the Maltese Falcon against the grand piano.

The financier proceeded to light his cigar with a $50 bill. To the surprise of Spiff, Jubee lit his with a $100 bill.

"Money doesn't impress me," Jubee said. "I want my brother back." Dud was throwing a large potted plant down upon the Maltese Falcon.

Morebucks relit his cigar with a $500 bill.

"I'm not in the adoption business. " Jubee then relit his cigar with a $1,000 bill, to the consternation of Spiff. Dud was drilling into the Maltese Falcon in an adjoining room.

"Neither am I," the lad replied, his eyes watering in the swirl of tobacco smoke.

Morebucks *now* used a $5,000 bill. "You can kiss my Fanny," he intoned. Dud was placing a lit stick of dynamite under the Maltese Falcon. He re-entered the room, closed the door, and placed his hands over his ears.

Jubee coolly lit a $10,000 bill. Spiff almost collapsed. "You can kiss her yourself if you do what I want."

There was a tremendous explosion, and when the smoke cleared the room was in shreds. Morebucks was dangling from the chandelier, defeated. "How old did you say your brother was?" he asked.

* * * * *

A short time later the ceiling had been propped up, and the papers were ready to be signed. "Wait a minute," said Jubee suddenly. "You'll have to adopt our sister, too."

"OUR SISTER?" exclaimed Spiff and Dud.

"How many of your relatives *are* there in that place," said Morebucks, glowering at the three of them.

"Only her," the lad replied. "You'll like her. She's a girl."

"Plus one sister," Morebucks sighed.

* * * * *

Several days later, the participants met again in the partially renovated room.

"This is Rosemary," said Jubee, introducing her to Morebucks.

"Her pupils are too big," the financier observed.

"You can have them removed. And this is Lucifer." The lad was still in ball and chain.

"That's 'Lucian,'" corrected Lucian.

"And this is the information you want on Little Orphan Fanny." Jubee placed an envelope on the table.

"I'm very dubious about having a boy around," said Morebucks doubtfully. "Even if it *is* for only five months."

"Aw, you'll get used to it," Jubee replied. "Punjoke and The Viper can help keep him in line."

"Well, I don't know…" The man started to sit down.

SPLAT!!

He jumped back up, then held aloft a whoopee cushion. Lucian laughed, and Punjoke and The Viper joined Morebucks in standing menacingly over the kids. Even the ropes were irate.

"Okay," Jubee said resignedly. "I'll take him back."

He lifted his brother's ball, and the four of them left. Morebucks then took Rosemary's hands.

"Can you say 'Arf'?" he inquired.

Just as the boys were coming down the steps, Rosemary threw open the

THE WONDERFUL EDISON TIME MACHINE

casement windows and joyfully trilled to a full symphonic orchestra: "Tomorrow, tomorrow, I love ya, tomorrow, you're only a day A-WAY." She hit a shattering high C as the boys piled in their ancient car and roared away.

CHAPTER TEN

MARKET MACHINATIONS

It was Friday, June 7, 1929. Someone was lighting Jubee's cigar, and that someone was Cardington, standing by his desk. Worthington and Greenwich applauded, and the latter began to cut a cake made in the form of a dollar sign, while Worthington uncorked a bottle of champagne. The liquid spurted freely, and Jubee, Spiff and Lucian, (who had requested Scumberry Juice) toasted one another and shook hands all around. They were all dressed like Wall Street tycoons.

Nearby, Dud was similarly attired. He held an open jeweler's case while the secretary was trying on a dazzling diamond lavalicrc. She looked at the boy with new-found admiration.

While eating cake, Jubee asked, "Did our new car arrive?"

"It's outside," said Worthington. "What a beauty."

"We're anxious to see it," said Spiff.

Cardington and the four boys stepped out onto the sidewalk. A few feet away was the truant officer, disguised as a cigar store Indian. The banker waved his hand and a magnificent Rolls-Royce town car glided up. Its driver saluted Jubee and extended him an invoice.

Jubee read it and then exclaimed, "$21,465 for a Rolls-Royce? These things don't come cheap, even in 1929." He signed the form, and immediately a large butterfly net engulfed him.

"White boy gettum caught." It was the truant officer.

THE WONDERFUL EDISON TIME MACHINE

"School's out, you dumbhead," Spiff said angrily.

"Ain't you never heard of *summer school*?" the man demanded.

Jubee was resigned. He rested his elbow on the car. "This could go on all summer."

Cardington took the officer's arm and led him aside. "Tell me, my good man, how much do you make a week?"

"Twenty-two fifty, and wot's it to ya?" the man replied. The banker propelled him further away. "Would you be open to a proposition?"

Dud freed Jubee from the net, then squarely faced him.

"Why didn't you buy an *American* car?"

"I *did*," the boy replied. "In the 1920s, Rolls-Royce built cars in Springfield, Massachusetts, as *well* as England. This *entire* car was built right here. It's as American as *apple pie*."

"In that case," Dud said, "let's get in."

Just as they did, the bank doors flew open and the secretary rushed out. "Yoo-hoo, Dudsy boy," she cried. "Wait for me. I had to get my coat."

"What you got you shouldn't cover," said Dud as she elbowed her way into the car. "Did 'ou miss me?" she pouted seductively.

Jubee turned his head, annoyed. "Who'll drive?" he said. The truant officer leaned back from the driver's seat. "At your pleasure, gentlemen," he said, and as the car moved off Dud pulled down the window shade.

Market Machinations

Sunday evening found the boys relaxing in their secret room. Spiff and Dud were tooting on some musical instruments, while Lucian played at a makeshift desk with his decoder ring.

Jubee closed the ledger he was working on.

"Well, tomorrow's the big day," he announced. "The day we start saving the Wizzer Automobile Company."

"Why tomorrow?" Spiff asked.

"You remember that oily guy we saw petting the stuffed dinosaur the first night we came here? He's the head of Ossificd Motors. Over the past two years he's been secretly borrowing millions of shares of my great-grandfather's company. Tomorrow he's going to start dumping those shares on the stock market to drive the price down and force great-grandfather into bankruptcy."

Lucian ran over to his older brother with a page of numbers, below which he had written letters.

"It says you should drink Ovaltine," Jubee told him.

"So what if the price goes down?" said Dud. "Your great-grandfather owns controlling interest. He doesn't *have* to sell his stock."

"That's just the trouble," Jubee said. "My great-grandfather no longer owns his stock. He's been living beyond his means for years and has pledged it all to the banks for loans. Once the stock starts going down, the banks will want additional security for their loans. They'll start sending great-grandfather 'margin calls.' Those are demands for cash or collateral to make up the difference between what they loaned on his stock and its current lower value.

"In my great-grandfather's case, the first margin call alone will be for forty million dollars, which he doesn't have, since he's already hocked everything except the house. And even if he could meet the first margin call, the next day he'd get another, and then another, as the stock keeps dropping. Sooner or later the bank would have to sell his stock. That would mean millions more shares dumped on the market for whatever they'd bring. In the ensuing panic

THE WONDERFUL EDISON TIME MACHINE

Wizzer stock will lose seventy percent of its value, and great-grandfather will be wiped out."

Lucian ran over with a new page of numbers, this time to Spiff.

"It says you should obey your mother and drink Ovaltine." Then to Jubee, "So how are you going to save his company?"

"Tomorrow I'll start *buying* Wizzer stock. Slowly at first. I don't want Ossified to know he's up against real money. The price will continue dropping, but the more he sells, the more I'll buy. Within a day or two he'll wonder where the support is coming from. He'll get desperate and throw more stock in. The price will keep on dropping, but it will *never* hit bottom, because I'll always be there: buying, buying — meeting him head-on, soaking it all up. By the time he realizes what's happened, it'll be too late. I'll have *bought* it all.

"Then the fun will *really* begin. Because Ossified has *borrowed* all the Wizzer stock he's selling — you can borrow stock, just like you can borrow money. But you have to *return* it. Ossified plans to sell all his borrowed stock to force the price down, then buy it back when the price is lower. That's called 'short selling.'"

Dud grabbed his groin. "Selling your shorts?" he agonized.

"A lot of people make money selling short in the stock market. First you find a stock you think is going to drop in value. Say it's selling for ninety dollars a share. You *borrow* a thousand shares from a stockbroker and immediately sell them for ninety thousand dollars. But you're obligated to return those thousand shares at a later date. So you wait a few months and pray to ten different gods that the stock will drop to say forty dollars a share. If it does, you buy them back for forty thousand dollars, return them to the owner, pay him a little interest, and pocket the fifty thousand dollar difference."

"Beats holding up Seven-Elevens," Spiff commented.

Lucian ran over to Dud with a final page of numbers.

"It says you should get laid and drink Ovaltine," he told the boy, then returned to Jubee. "What if the borrowed stock goes up?"

MARKET MACHINATIONS

"Then the short-seller takes a loss. The stock has 'gone long,' meaning it's gone up. If he sold the borrowed stock at ninety, and has to replace it at a hundred and forty, he *loses* fifty dollars a share, or fifty thousand dollars. It's a gamble."

"I'd rather shoot craps in Vegas," Dud observed.

"Ossified will be *pimping* in Las Vegas when I get through with him. Once he's sold his Wizzer stock I'll drive the price so high it will cost him two hundred million dollars to replace it. When the smoke clears, *I* should have control of Wizzer."

"Should have?" said Spiff. "Is there a problem?"

"I don't know," his friend replied. "Mr. Cardington contacted me today. He sounded worried. He wants us to meet him tomorrow at the Harbor Club. He says it's about something we didn't foresee."

CHAPTER ELEVEN

FOLLOW THE CALL

With a musical flourish the silvery curtains of the Harbor Club swept back to reveal a tacky African stage setting with fifteen white people in blackface beating on tom-toms. A sign at the side announced "The Hottentots in BONGO ON THE CONGO." They began to sing the popular Broadway song, although their interpretation was both racist and degrading.

> "In Bongo, it's on the Congo,
> And oh boy, what a spot.
> Quite full of things delightful,
> And few that are not.
> The native dances are worth some glances;
> You can't beat them anywhere."

The audience, consisting mostly of balding men amid women of temporary acquaintance, responded lustily with jeers and catcalls, and signaled waiters for more champagne.

Jubee, Spiff and Dud peered out at the performers through a part in the beaded curtain. Suddenly Jubee looked startled. He frowned and looked back into their alcove. He saw a half-eaten dish of ice cream and a box of Animal Crackers by a pushed-back chair. The boy made quickly for the door.

Jubee thrust his way determinedly through the drunken, boisterous crowd. He stopped at a table where three thinly-clad women noted more for

FOLLOW THE CALL

their availability than their virtue were being entertained by a pint-sized sugar daddy who was smoking a large cigar and waving a fistful of cash. It was Lucian, fallen again. Jubee scooped him up and propelled him off, to the plaintive wails of his new-found diaphanous friends.

Back in the alcove, Lucian was pushed into his chair. He brightened momentarily, due to something the ladies had said.

"Jubee, if Daddy was makin' it with a stork, shouldn't I be able to fly?"

Scowls were his only reply, so he began moodily playing with his Animal Crackers. Cardington entered and sat down, and the older boys gathered around him.

"Things went well today," he announced. "You picked up two million shares of stock, and we've barely even started."

"So what's the problem?" Spiff inquired.

The banker now looked thoughtful. "There's a large block of stock that's crucial to your plan. You've got to get it, or you'll never gain control of Wizzer. And it's held by a man who's sworn that he'll never sell — a man named Mark Willoughby."

"Uncle — you mean George Willoughby's *older brother*?" asked Jubee.

"Yes, the banker said. "The founder of Wizzer Automobile left the company equally to *both* his sons. And the sons are as different as *day* and *night*."

Dud spoke up. "What's this Mark guy like?" And Cardington began a curious tale.

"He and his wife Vera live in a towering

gothic mansion on the outskirts of town. Though surrounded with splendor, they have rejected the temptations of the temporal world and have devoted themselves entirely to the spiritual…"

As he spoke, there came the repressive, sinister sound of organ music. There was a long baronial hall at the end of which was a landing with a long, narrow dinner table, severely set. The two Willoughbys sat at opposite ends, both frozen as popsicles. Behind them loomed an immense arched window, somber with approaching twilight. Two black servants approached with silver-covered trays. The lids were lifted, revealing a very spartan meal. Mark nodded his approval, and the food was set before them.

Cardington continued, the boys all eyes on him. "The immense income they derive from their Wizzer stock has enabled them to establish a world-wide empire of religious missions dedicated to helping poor and helpless colored people wherever they are, as long as they're not in this country."

"That's only fair," Spiff acknowledged.

There came a group of igloos at the North Pole, a larger cathedral made of snow within their midst. There was a group of straw huts on the African veldt, a larger one of thatch made to resemble a basilica. And lastly, one of mud, its Gaudi-like spirals rising above the sun-baked soil of suburban Timbuktu.

"The Willoughbys have long been highly regarded for their many charitable undertakings. But over the years they have become increasingly gullible, and are today an easy prey for every religious charlatan in town."

Mark and Vera were still at dinner. Suddenly an old-fashioned radio with a large curved horn in the middle of the table crackled into life.

"Emergency! This is radio station WFDF coming to you by short-wave from the Emirate of Umbrellastand. The foogeywoogies have again stormed the mission compound and are taking turns hacking at Reverend Sabine." *There came the sounds of mortal combat.*

Four young men were in the woods outside the mansion. They were

FOLLOW THE CALL

broadcasting on a make-shift radio, and making a terrific clamor.

"He's up; he's down. He's fighting for his life. Mrs. Sabine has been captured. They're carrying her away to a fate worse than death. She's smiling, thinking of her martyrdom. Oh, if only General Gordon could get here in time. But his army can't pay the ferry toll to cross the Tarbush River."

Mark angrily choked the radio horn. "Smite the heathen," he cried. "Slay the unrighteous! Help is on the way."

"Make it in small bills," the radio gasped.

Mark pressed a button, took a wrapped package of bills from a stack on the table, and gave it to the approaching butler. This worthy carried it to the front door, where he was confronted by three of the young men, all hastily dressed as ministers. One even struggled with a large Bible. They accepted the money from the disdainful butler and genuflected gravely as the door was slammed on them.

THE WONDERFUL EDISON TIME MACHINE

They then ran gaily to a nearby flivver filled with flappers. One of the boys waved the packet of money at the nubile maidens, while another opened the Bible and took out several flasks of gin.

The Willoughbys waited anxiously by the radio. Cautiously, it creaked again to life.

"The money arrived just in time," it breathlessly announced. "General Gordon has stormed the city. They're putting Reverend Sabine back together again. Mrs. Sabine has been saved. She's no longer smiling. It's a miracle!"

Mark and Vera collapsed in each other's arms as the radio went dead. In the distance, three black servants were observing by the drapery. They shook their heads, then entered the kitchen. They sat down with six or seven others to the same bleak meal, while one of the women sewed a patch on a threadbare chauffeur's uniform.

*   *   *   *   *

Dud asked, "So how do we con the stock out of him?"

"We can't," said Cardington. "It's held in trust for charitable works. What we need are the *voting rights*. I've just found out that Mark and Vera have been talked into taking a *five-year* tour of their foreign missions. And that while they're gone, the dividends and voting rights to the Wizzer stock are to be signed over to the FTC."

"The Federal Trade Commission?" Jubee asked.

"The Follow the Call religious movement. Haven't you seen their followers around town collecting money? The Willoughbys are only waiting for a sign from heaven, and enough helium for their dirigible, before they sign the document. Once they do, you're *through*."

Jubee pondered for a moment. "Can't we bribe the FTC? Let them *keep* the dividends. All we want are the voting rights. Offer them a million dollars."

"You don't understand," replied the banker. "The FTC is not a *real* religious organization. It's a phony outfit set up by Ossified Motors to trick Mark out of his stock."

FOLLOW THE CALL

"What can we do?" said Jubee.

"If only we could infiltrate the FTC, find out more about them, but there's very little time. Ossified plans to fake the sign, and say that it's from heaven."

Spiff was getting an idea. "Who's the head of this Follow the Call racket?" he asked Cardington.

"Two ex-radio evangelists," the man replied, "called *Fred and Flora Flummox*."

CHAPTER TWELVE

SPIFF BECOMES A SPY

A couple of days later the kitchen door of the Mark Willoughby mansion burst open and Flora Flummox swept in, followed by her husband, Fred. She was a shrewish, heavily made-up woman, whose lineage and usual profession could be traced directly back to ancient Babylon. He was cherubic and somewhat tipsy, more unacquainted with sin than against it. The black household staff rose, and Fred headed directly for the cookie jar. There his hand encountered a mousetrap, and he sucked his injured thumb in innocent bewilderment while Flora beckoned imperiously for a side door to be opened.

Through it stepped a line of clean-cut white youths, all carrying FTC donation cans. As they passed by Flora, she appraised each one sternly. One of the girls, safely past her, directed a coquettish smile at Fred, who reacted with dread and fascination.

Last in line was Spiff. Flora was displeased, but he grinned and rattled his canister, revealing several coins. With resignation, she let him pass.

*   *   *   *   *

Later that afternoon Spiff was standing on a street corner attempting to collect money. He darted out at several people, only to be rebuffed. Dejected, he ran beside a pedestrian.

"Donate to Follow the Call?" he cajoled. "God will like you."

Ignored, Spiff grabbed a discarded booklet from a nearby ledge and continued.

SPIFF BECOMES A SPY

"I'll throw in a copy of *The Watchtower.* Twice the protection."

The man moved on, and Spiff spotted another one.

"Donate to Follow the Call? Send a colored kid to camp?" The man continued on. "A CONCENTRATION CAMP?" called Spiff. The man turned and plunked a coin in the boy's can.

"I'll be damned if I'll say *that* all day," Spiff thought. "There's *got* to be a better way. Who do I know that's dumber than hell and has a lot of money?"

* * * * *

When Spiff opened the door to their secret room an hour later, he was met with a blizzard of paper money. It was almost knee deep, and he had to fight his way inside. Dud was sitting in a chair in front of a fan atop a box. Lucian was standing on another box pouring out a basketful of currency. Bills were scattered everywhere, and Dud let out a deep sigh of relief.

"I can see you're accomplishing a lot," said Spiff drily.

Dud closed his eyes in contentment. "Can I help it if there's no air-conditioning in 1929?"

Spiff began stuffing wads of money in his can. "HEY!" cried Dud, opening his eyes. "Hey yourself," said Spiff, and continued with his stuffing.

* * * * *

Twilight on this auspicious day found Spiff eating a simple meal at the communal kitchen table in the Mark Willoughby mansion. One of the white Follow the Call boys entered from outside. He shook his red collection can at Spiff, and it made a healthy rattle. Spiff obligingly lifted and shook his own can. It made no sound. The white boy gave a silent laugh and continued on through a door into the dining area where animated voices could be heard. Spiff returned to eating.

Another boy came through, and the sound of his can promised even greater wealth. And then a third came in, this one with *two* collection cans, which he manipulated like castanets.

"Cha-cha-cha," commented Spiff.

THE WONDERFUL EDISON TIME MACHINE

The black servants taking food into the adjoining room had viewed these proceedings with alarm. They conferred among themselves, then dug into their pockets. Pearl, their acknowledged leader, approached, followed by the others. To Spiff's surprise, they all dropped coins in his can.

Reverend Honeysuckle, an elderly black minister, then entered from outside. He was carrying some frayed sheet music which he distributed to the servants. One of them opened a side door to a small rear quarter where there was an old piano and some chairs. The blacks congregated there and prepared to rehearse.

Spiff looked at them, then turned as the robust sound of the FTC recruitment song came through the closed doorway into the dining area.

SPIFF BECOMES A SPY

He turned back as the quiet but growing chords of the Negro spiritual "I've Seen the City of The Lord" came from the servants' quarters.

The two songs complemented each other, but the spiritual built in strength. Then the dining room door swung open and the FTC members, led by Flora, filed in. Still singing, they arranged themselves behind the evangelist as she sat down at an accounting table. Her husband Fred brought up the rear, struggling with a large calculating machine.

The whites approached and dumped the contents of their cans upon the table, making little mounds of coins. Then all eyes turned to Spiff. The blacks had filed back into the room, and the two songs hung breathless in the air.

Spiff took his collection can to the table. There was derision in the eyes of the FTC members. Spiff upended the can and tapped it. Six or seven coins dropped out. There was a beginning swell of laughter. Spiff tapped the can again, harder, and a large, tightly-compacted wad of currency fell to the table. A stunned gasp filled the room. Spiff then dug into his pockets and pulled out an even greater accumulation of bills.

To the thunderous final peals of "I've Seen the City of the Lord," the Flummoxes beamed broadly and extended Spiff a multi-colored ribbon, while the other whites reacted in dismay.

*   *   *   *   *

Later that evening the same song was winding down, but this time in Reverend Honeysuckle's plain, impoverished church. The singers were the same, and Spiff was there, dressed in an inexpensive black suit. He looked around at the parishioners, many of them aged and worn. When the music ended, Pearl smiled at him from the choir stall as Reverend Honeysuckle rose to speak.

CHAPTER THIRTEEN

THE SIGN FROM HEAVEN

Several days later Spiff was in their secret room happily affixing his fifth ribbon to a wooden Follow the Call plaque and singing to himself:

"In Bongo, it's on the Congo,
And oh boy what a spot.
Girls that are hot;
Real hot to trot…"

Jubee looked on in disgust as Spiff stepped back to admire his display. "Five more of these and I'm assured a place in the white man's heaven," he said.

Jubee could control himself no longer. "Do you suppose you could put your salvation on hold long enough to show me some progress? *This is costing me money!*"

"Stay cool, Dad," Spiff replied. "Tomorrow the big enchilada himself is taking the stock certificate out of the family vault to pray over. It's my job to see it never gets returned."

"Well, don't be too cocky," Jubee said in retort. "This isn't your usual set of hubcaps."

"It's all the same to a *pro!*" Spiff bragged.

*   *   *   *   *

At noon the next day Spiff was sitting in the kitchen of the Mark Willoughby mansion drinking a glass of milk. He looked out the window and saw several automobiles being shunted to the back. He gazed sharply around him and then, unobserved, disappeared through a side door.

A celestial sigh, emanating from the ramparts at some far-off paradise, greeted him as he entered the icy, embalmed rooms of the main part of the house. Like a warrior from an aboriginal age, he slipped softly through its rich, unused furnishings. He stopped at the sound of distant voices.

Mark and Vera were in the entryway greeting three somber ministers as servants relieved them of their hats. Flora Flummox was also present, giving worried glances towards the door.

Mark, with trembling hands, held up a framed stock certificate.

"Gentlemen! Heaven continues to test our endurance and withhold the sign we so desperately seek. We will pray for guidance before the portrait of Herkimer and Henrietta Hoot, the martyred founders of our movement.

"Vera has with her the decanter of water taken from the River Jordan by the Hoots almost fifty years ago, when they paused on the road to Damascus to make their vows to God.

"Just as this jug remained forever with them, always miraculously full, through all their travails in setting up the world's greatest missionary chain, so does it remind us all today of the fullness of our faith and the correctness of our path."

Spiff, crouching behind a couch, heard a servant giving instructions to another. "They're meeting in the library." The boy looked wildly about, then saw a convenient standing sign which said "Library." He quickly sprinted across the room and entered through its heavily carved doorway.

He found himself in a treasure room pungent with the smell of age-old leather bindings and aglow with gold and silver objects plundered from the greatest cities of the Renaissance. To his right was a life-size statue of a blackamoor, naked from the waist up, holding aloft a candelabra of electric lights. Ahead of him was a long refectory table graced by a Cellini salt cellar, beyond which was a mammoth fireplace Hearst was out-bid on. Above it was another portrait of the founder of the Wizzer Automobile Company.

THE SIGN FROM HEAVEN

To its right was a shrine to the martyred Hoots, including a portrait of them in a cannibal pot attributed to Grant Wood. Henrietta was wearing an old-fashioned bonnet, and Herkimer had on a pith helmet. Beside them was the jug of water from the River Jordan.

A lighted cabinet held mementoes of their distinguished career: a coconut, an ostrich egg, a Coca-Cola bottle, some photos of the Hoots with native chieftains, ivory salt and pepper shakers, an autographed picture of Tarzan, a catsup bottle, a menu card with "The Hoots" written in, some reading glasses, and a pair of false teeth.

Spiff's swift perusal was short-lived. There came the sound of approaching voices, and panic filled his face. He desperately looked for a place to hide. There was none. The voices were getting closer. He spied a small end table with a red velvet covering. He whipped the cloth off, hastily removed the shade from the table's lamp, glanced fearfully at the doorway, and began to rip away his clothes.

Voices, then the group of visitors entered the room. Flora was still looking doubtfully behind. Vera put the decanter on the refectory table, and Mark did likewise with the stock certificate. They all then proceeded downwind to the Hoot portrait, and did not notice Spiff, who was posing as an identical blackamoor on the other side of the doorway. He was now naked except for the table covering around his loins. Above his head he held the shadeless lamp fixture. With sweat appearing on his forehead, his eyes followed the group. Then they fixated on the framed certificate. Spiff grinned as in the distance Mark began to pray.

"Oh Lord, hear us this day as we stand in tribulation before the sacred portrait of Herkimer and Henrietta Hoot, the founders of our ministry. Know that we seek Your divine guidance before undertaking an exhausting tour of our foreign missions located around the globe in the most arduous of climes."

As he prayed, Fred Flummox skidded into the room, somewhat inebriated and smoking a cigarette. Flora gestured for him to dispose of it.

Mark continued on, not one to let God off easily. "Know also our intention to leave the keys to our temporal kingdom to Fred and Flora Flummox, spiritual leaders of the Follow the Call crusade, who, during our extended absence, will oversee our missionary empire, at the same time abstaining themselves from all things worldly so they may share in the same privations we will be experiencing in the field."

Fred looked around for a place to hide his cigarette. He spotted the figure of Spiff and, lowering the boy's jaw, thrust his cigarette inside. He then closed Spiff's mouth and rushed off to join the others. Smoke curled out of Spiff's ears, and the light he was holding began to flicker.

Oblivious, Mark continued his tirade to the Trinity.

"And know always it is our sacred duty to proclaim Your word throughout the world, so that all unfortunate colored people, who at this *very moment* are writhing in the agony of a fiery hell, may partake of Your healing power and accept salvation."

Spiff fell to the floor, his throat on fire, and did an agonizing breakdance. He silently pounded the floor, then rose and did a stilted Pharaonic Egyptian dance. His loin cloth came off, revealing his 1929 BVD's. After several other painful contortions, including an Al Jolson "Mammy" pose, he spotted the decanter with the waters of the River Jordan and gulped it down. He let out a

THE SIGN FROM HEAVEN

tremendous silent breath of satisfaction as the fire was extinguished, and shakily regained his stance just as the prayer came to an end.

"We unworthy recipients of Your eternal largesse await Your sign. Amen!"

The group reapproached the center of the room. Vera spied the overturned decanter, and in shock cried out.

"It's empty! The waters of the River Jordan are gone!"

"It's the *sign*," cried Flora, who had never missed a trick since she was sixteen. "Your faith is empty! It must be refilled through new and greater sacrifice. It's *God's will!*"

Mark joined in, excitedly. "It's the *miracle* we've been waiting for. We'll *go* on the tour of our foreign missions. And we'll *sign* our charter over to the FTC. We'll sign it at a great revival leave-taking this Saturday, where we'll re-enact the martyrdom of Herkimer and Henrietta Hoot *for all the world to see.*"

With that they all rushed out. Last to go was Fred Flummox, who attempted to retrieve his cigarette by putting his arm down Spiff's throat. The boy bit him, and when again alone in the room, he burped.

CHAPTER FOURTEEN

THE GREAT HOOTENANNY

Saturday found the Mark Willoughby estate festooned for the festivities. The great leave-taking had arrived. The back lawn contained a number of multicolored tents, a stage, and a viewing stand where notables were gathering. There were reporters and newsreel cameramen, and even a band positioning to play. Papier maché palm trees were being placed around a large iron pot in last-minute preparations.

Floating over the field was a giant dirigible, a large painted cross on its side with interconnected "M" and "V" initials. Below it was a sign: "Zanzibar or Bust." Six stout ropes moored the airship to the ground, and an ornate basket decorated with bunting had been lowered to the stand.

Inside a tent, twenty or so white men, mostly from the Harbor Club entertainment committee, were putting on black face and African costumes. They were having a rollicking time.

Meanwhile, in the Mark Willoughby mansion there came a heavy pounding on the front door. Vera entered the foyer and passed the sheeted furniture. She was carrying a small suitcase.

"Where *can* the servants be?" she exclaimed, distraught. "We didn't fire *all* of them."

She opened the door. Spiff was standing there, disguised as a South Sea chieftain, an inflated inner tube beneath his grass skirt and a bone tied in his hair. He was accompanied by a witch doctor and several dozen warriors,

THE GREAT HOOTENANNY

courtesy of Mark's household staff and Reverend Honeysuckle's church.

"You, skinny lady with no bazooms," spoke Spiff authoritatively. "Tell chief of big hut King Bongo here; come long distance with sick, sick heart."

"King Bongo? From the Sandwich Islands?" Vera was astonished. "We're *sending* you Doctor Mayo."

"Hold the Mayo. Me sick about native cousins on Baloney Islands *next* to Sandwich Islands. *They have never heard the Word.*"

"Really? My husband will be so concerned. Just go around back." Joyfully Vera closed the door. "Oh, the Lord is with us all today," she informed the wallpaper.

In the staging tent the white cannibal king and the others were putting on their final makeup. Then a flap was thrown back and Spiff and his warriors entered. The whites stared incredulously. These looked like *real* cannibals. Silently, the blacks inspected the whites, wiping off their paint and bending their rubber arrows. Within moments the whites had turned and fled.

Pearl, one of the invaders, then peered out a narrow slit in the canvas. There came the sound of cheers.

"The ceremony is beginning," she said. "Mark has signed the document."

Outside, Fred and Flora were bound within the iron pot, below which was a simulated fire. Two "black" guards looked on hungrily while a cook cut onion slices into the pot. A worker had just placed the signed Willoughby document on a nearby stand.

An unseen announcer began to pontificate.

"And it came to pass that in a jungle clearing, after a lifetime of selfless devotion to the lower species, the lives of Herkimer and Henrietta Hoot were drawing to a close."

There were groans from the audience.

Chanting now came from an angelic chorus:

"No words of anguish crossed their lips.
With Christ they'd cast their lot.

THE WONDERFUL EDISON TIME MACHINE

Now was their time of martyrdom;
Parboiled in a pot.

"With only moments left to go
(The menu called for rare),
There came the sound of angels' wings
Which filled the noontime air.

"And on that day, so long ago,
'Mid onions gently stirred,
They saw the golden fields of God,
And this is what they heard…"

As the music paused, expectant, Spiff burst out upon the stage, followed by his warriors. As other blacks scared off the angelic white singers, he began to sing a wild savage song. His cohorts took the chorus:

Spiff's Song

"In a far-off land, by a far-off sea
Lives a group of happy natives in harmony.
They don't wear any clothing,
And they don't know sin.
And they spend the tropic hours
Drinking coconut gin.

"They never, ever heard the Word,
So all they do is do it.
If you could get them to sequester
With the holy Book of Esther
That would surely bring a very quick end to it.

THE GREAT HOOTENANNY

"In this pagan society sex has great variety,
And anywhere is just the place to spoon.
If the beach is filled with figgers,
They make love in their outriggers,
And are lulled to sleep by waves beneath the moon."

While Spiff belted out his song, Fred and Flora, still ensconced in the cannibal pot, gaped in astonishment as their two black-face guardians were hooked offstage and replaced by real blacks, who proceeded to gag them. A garden hose then filled the pot with water as *real* paper and kindling were placed around its base. The Flummoxes looked down in horror as the material was ignited.

"They never, ever heard the Word,
So all they do is do it.
If their faith is but one granule,
Read them the Book of Samuel.
That would surely bring a very quick end to it.

"Now it's plain as plain can be
That they're damned eternally,
And missionaries are what they're really needin'.
Send professional and lay ones
(But don't send any gay ones)
And put an end to this licentious Eden.

"They never, ever heard the Word,
So all they do is do it.
If natives want your bod to probe,
Preach to them the Book of Job.
That would surely bring a very quick end to it."

THE WONDERFUL EDISON TIME MACHINE

Meanwhile, the white deposed cannibal king, spear in hand, had snuck around the tent. He saw that the Flummoxes were squirming in panic as the water in the pot began to froth. A guard stepped over to the mounted charter and removed it. While Spiff continued to sing, the guard held it before Fred and indicated he should sign. The two evangelists, sweat rolling down their faces, eagerly nodded "yes." Another guard dipped his hand into the water, grimaced, and released Fred's bonds as the choir from Honeysuckle's church joined in.

"Drop anchor in their golden bay
Beside the rose-toned reef;
Bring Bible tracts which clearly show
How idleness brings grief.
Build them a school and a factory;
Convince them that all things denied
Makes purer the soul at the endtime
When it helps to be sanctified.

"They never, ever heard the Word,
So all they do is do it.
If they ask you for coitus,
Speak of Samson and Delitus.
That would surely bring a very quick end to it.

"Keep them away from the fish-filled sea
And the warmth of a loving sun.
Promise instead a great afterlife
Which is theirs when they finally succumb.

"And when they lay dying a miserable death
Far removed from the earth and the sky,
Sprinkle some water and mumble some words,
And hope they don't ask of you why."

THE GREAT HOOTENANNY

The white cannibal king raised his spear just as Spiff reached the song's climax. Fred signed the document as two blacks snuck out and attached chains to metal loops on each side of the cauldron.

"They never, ever heard the Word,
So all they do is do it.
The most hardened south seas strumpet
Can be saved by Gabriel's trumpet.
That would surely bring a very quick end to it."

The cannibal king threw his spear, and Spiff was punctured. The inner tube made an obscene sound as it and Spiff deflated. Black workers cut the mooring

lines of the dirigible, and its wicker basket began to rise. The Willoughbys grabbed the railing and waved goodbye. The cannibal king charged across the stage, intent on saving the Flummoxes, but Spiff tripped him.

There came the sound of rattling chains, and the Flummoxes looked at Spiff and then at each other with renewed terror. Then the chains yanked upward, and the pot was raised aloft. Everyone ran across the lawn shouting goodbye while the band played "Happy Days Are Here Again."

Jubee, Dud and Lucian raced through the crowd toward Spiff. They laughed, whooped and embraced the boy. Then they looked skyward. The mammoth airship had slowly turned, as the pot containing the Flummoxes swung below.

Up above, the Willoughbys were waiting in the ship's cabin. The pot was hauled aboard, and the two evangelists were spilled out. Shakily, they stood.

Mark eyed them with fanaticism. "It is the will of God. You are to share our privations for the next five years. *We shall pray.*" Behind him a dozen somber parsons began to hum a single note. The Flummoxes fainted dead away.

* * * * *

Later that evening Spiff, Dud, Jubee and the others were in the Willoughby library seated around the refectory table, which was piled high with hotdogs and bowls of popcorn. Jubee was downing a soft drink.

"Well, let's see it," he said, pleased. Spiff nodded and the framed charter was passed to him. Instantly Jubee cried aloud.

"The Flummoxes endorsed it all right, but it's still made out to the FTC. It's *no good.*"

Pearl, who was present, begged to differ. "Honey, what do you think 'FTC' stands for?"

"Follow the Call," said Jubee.

"Uh-uh!" the woman said. "It stands for Flint Technical College." Cheers came from everywhere.

The Great Hootenanny

Spiff explained hastily. "You'll get all the *voting* rights to the Wizzer stock, but the *dividends* will go to build a school."

"Flint *needs* a technical college," added Reverend Honeysuckle. "Especially one for colored people."

"But I want whites in it too," said Spiff, strongly.

Pearl voiced concern. "Whites in a colored school? They won't come."

"Maybe they will if you ask them," Spiff replied. "If this town's to have a future, it'd better welcome everyone." There were more cheers.

"Suits me fine," said Jubee. "And here's something from the three of us, for all your help." He extended a paper tube.

Pearl unrolled it and exclaimed in astonishment.

"It's the *deed* to the *Harbor Club*." The other blacks crowded around.

"No more 'Bongo on the Congo,'" said Dud.

"But that's Slugsy's place!" exclaimed one man in shock.

"Not anymore," said Jubee. "I got the mayor to close it down."

"How did you do that?" asked another.

"By paying him more than Slugsy does." Jubee stood. "It's all yours now. You can make a *real* place of it. A place where the *decent* people of Flint will want to go. With food and music and… well, here's a check to get you started."

The boy handed a large check to Pearl, who read it and then jumped up and kissed him. Reverend Honeysuckle picked it up.

"How much is it for?" "How's it made out?" cried the onlookers.

Reverend Honeysuckle spoke dramatically.

"It's for *fifty thousand dollars*, and it's made out to…"

*　*　*　*　*

One week later the Harbor club was being renovated. Its roofline revealed the well-known six-foot letters that read HARBOR CLUB. A worker guided down six new letters, and the sign now read…PEARL'S HARBOR CLUB.

CHAPTER FIFTEEN

THE SECRET IN THE GREENHOUSE

The warm dog days of summer were now upon them, and five days later Jubee and Margaret were taking tea in a gazebo on her parents' estate. It was late afternoon, and revelers behind them were setting off fireworks under a banner that read "Happy 4th of July — Detroit Symphony Here Tonight." The boy had just opened a suitcase filled with stock certificates and was flipping through them.

"You and your brother now own controlling interest in Wizzer. Look: five thousand shares, three thousand shares, twenty thousand shares. All in your names. No one can take it away from you now."

Margaret was overwhelmed with gratitude. "Oh, I didn't think you could do it. You really must be rich. How can David and I ever thank you?"

"By running a good company," Jubee replied. "Think of your descendants. I mean, you've got to keep the company for the future. For posterity."

Behind them Lucian, dressed as a Revolutionary War soldier, ran past holding a huge lighted firecracker. Dud was chasing him. They disappeared only to reappear, this time Dud running with the firecracker and Lucian in hot pursuit. The little boy now had a musket, which he stopped to fire just as distant cries were heard:

"*Not in the pool! NOT IN THE...!*"

Lucian's musket (actually a pop-gun) went off, followed by an earthshaking blast and a drenching shower of water and bathing suits. Lucian exited, satisfied.

THE SECRET IN THE GREENHOUSE

Margaret was unperturbed. "Mother and Father will be so happy when I tell them."

"No, don't tell them," Jubee said. "Keep it *our* secret. There is a crash com- I mean, things change. Your parents don't control Wizzer anymore. Let them keep their never-ending party for a few more months. That way they'll stay out of our way while we reorganize the company."

"Well, whatever you think best. But we'll never forget this," the girl replied. "And *I* have a present for *you*. Something…Oh, my brother's home. Let me tell *him!* He was so worried when the stock was going down." She withdrew a bundle of stock certificates and snapped the suitcase shut as a butler approached. Smiling, she addressed him.

"Oh, Meddlesome – will you clear these things away and take this suitcase to my room? Hide it under the bed."

Jubee laughed. "I hope you have a big bed. There are eight more suitcases just like that one."

David and Meadowcroft, the earnest young man who was in love with Margaret's older sister, were just stepping from their car. Meadowcroft spied three brightly-colored canisters some thirty inches high which stood a few feet away. They were labeled "Honorable Blueprint Disposal" and each had a single Japanese character printed on its side. The canisters glided over with hopeful expressions.

"They're back again," Meadowcroft observed.

He and David stuck some blueprints down a hole on top of the canisters and were rewarded with a whirring sound and some unintelligible words. The three canisters then bowed in thanks and scurried off, bumping into each other as they passed the prohibition agents checking cars. An upturned orange crate held the agents' confiscated contraband, including issues of *Ballyhoo, Film Fun,* and several hip flasks.

Margaret excitedly drew David away while Jubee approached Meadowcroft.

THE WONDERFUL EDISON TIME MACHINE

"What's with the canisters?" he inquired.

"Oh, they belong to the Krockashitas. They're foreign industrial spies posing as junkmen. They're always trying to steal Flint's automotive secrets, but everybody's on to them. Today we gave their robots plans for Flint's first sludge plant, built in 1864. I'd like to see what they can build with *that*."

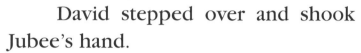

David stepped over and shook Jubee's hand.

"Margaret's told me what you've done. Words can't express our thanks. It means the factory won't be closed. It means the workers can keep their jobs. And it means we can tell you our secret."

At this word, Meddlesome paused in taking Margaret's suitcase up the steps, while one of the canisters returned and nuzzled David's pants.

Margaret's brother continued. "For the past year Otis and I have been working on a top-secret project, something we believe will revolutionize the automobile industry. I've asked the family to come down to the greenhouse after supper. It's a *real* surprise, and we want you to come too."

Jubee and Margaret responded with enthusiasm.

*   *   *   *   *

That evening an odd assortment of individuals gathered by the greenhouse door. It included not only Jubee and Margaret, but also Imogene, her older sister, who was dressed as Betsy Ross, her boyfriend Lord Doomsbury, who was dressed like George Arliss, and her parents, who were dressed as George and Martha Washington.

Making sure they weren't observed, David admitted the group and led them through the shadowed foliage to a brilliantly-lighted workroom, in the center of which was a gleaming new Wizzer sport phaeton. Meadowcroft turned from working on it, but only had eyes for Imogene. His assistant, a young mute named Derby, looked on proudly.

George chuckled with amusement. "So *this* is how you've been wasting the firm's money."

"It's an all-new Wizzer, Dad, the Wizzer PLAYBOY," David quickly said. "Double the cylinders, silent-shift transmission, hydraulic brakes, independent wheel suspension, automatic lubrication. Even all-round safety glass. It's all I've ever dreamed about. And speed…"

"Now son, be practical," the boy's father broke in. "It's very pretty, I'll admit, and probably very fast. But we've *already got* a good car. We've hardly changed our STOVE BOLT SIX in the past twenty years, and people are still buying it. They'll *always* buy it, unless some damn fool gives them something better."

David strove to be patient. "Dad! Cadillac is building a sixteen-cylinder car. 1930 is just around the corner. People want things *modern*. Even Ford had to junk the Model T and replace it with the A."

"Yes, and Henry had to close his plant *six months* to retool," George replied. "And Cadillac can *have* their V-sixteen. It's only for prestige. They'll never make a dime on it."

"But Dad…"

"People would still be driving curved-dash Oldsmobiles and be *happy* to have them, if it weren't for dreamers like yourself. Our car goes just as fast as people *ought* to go. There's no need to *improve* things. Things are fine just as they are. Next you'll be wanting us to *unionize* our plants."

Derby had approached Meadowcroft and was making a curved vertical movement with his hands. Meadowcroft was momentarily puzzled.

Margaret strove to be helpful. "He wants a Coke."

"He wants a girl," Jubee interpreted.

"He wants a bumper," said Meadowcroft, who took a long, wrapped package from a nearby pile and gave it to the mute.

THE WONDERFUL EDISON TIME MACHINE

Imogene and Lord Doomsbury had been snickering together. Margaret turned and addressed the Englishman. "Lord Doomsbury, they make cars in England. What do you think?"

Rattled, Lord Doomsbury adjusted his monocle.

"Dash it all; stiff upper lip, no sticky wicket, you know."

In desperation David turned again to his father. "She'll be ready for a trial run in three weeks. Then it can be our star attraction at the New York Auto Show…"

His father stood aghast. "If you take that car to New York, you'll destroy the company. No one will want the old Wizzer. Think how your grandfather would feel." He put his arm imploringly around his son.

"If you *really* want to help the company, do something *practical*. Design a new seal for our radiator cap." He then turned to his wife. "And now, Marian, we'd better get back to our guests."

"Why don't you bring back the Wizzer PIDDLE?" she gurgled. "It was a lovely little car. And it was very successful."

"Yes," George allowed, as they turned to go. "The PIDDLE made a splash."

Jubee and Margaret trailed the others out, then stopped by some windows.

"Next time they should dress like Neanderthals," Jubee said.

"Poor David," his girlfriend replied. "He's worked so hard. But you've made it possible for him to continue. Now we can tool up for the new Wizzer no matter *what* Daddy says. And when the Playboy's shown at the New York Auto Show, it'll be a *sensation*."

"Yes," Jubee agreed. "David's giving the company what it needs. Something new, something *better*. That should always be your goal."

Margaret moved closer to the boy. "Do you know we raise *mistletoe* in here? It's right above us."

"Oh, corn! Do they have *that* here?"

Margaret struggled to imitate Clara Bow. "And I've got something for you," she cooed. "Remember? I told you I had a present."

THE SECRET IN THE GREENHOUSE

The girl opened her purse and extended an object to Jubee. He turned it over several times, and it flashed in the outside light. It was a carrying-case for Jujubes, shaped and engraved exactly like the famous box of candy.

"It's…it's…solid gold," the boy confided. "I can tell."

Jubee looked at Margaret just as the Detroit Symphony began playing Handel's "Royal Fireworks." There came the sounds of a colossal fireworks display, and its multicolored reflection struck the faces of both teenagers as he took Margaret in his arms and kissed her.

Their hearts soared with the velvet tracery of the Roman candles in the sky, and they did not notice Meddlesome, who was spying on them through the windows.

CHAPTER SIXTEEN

MUSICAL CHAIRS

Now that the boys were millionaires, Jubee felt they should begin to act the part. He was unsure how to accomplish this, but he felt it probably involved a lavish and continual expenditure of money. So he kept a basketful in the trunk of the Rolls and dipped into it whenever necessary.

But the primordial Flint of 1929 provided few of the real amenities of life, such as comic books, video games, skateboards, boom boxes and Big Macs. So most of his expenditures went for *looking* the part, and they all now sported jeweled walking sticks, top hats, gold watch fobs, shoes with spats, and fur coats, which they wore in even the hottest weather.

Jubee had accoutered them all at Smith-Bridgman's Department Store on West Kearsley Street, and when he saw what he had done, he pronounced it good. Had the next day been the seventh, he would have rested, but since it wasn't he decided they should go for a drive.

Vanity plates had not yet been invented, but Jubee had enough for the entire car. He entered it with hauteur, along with Spiff, Dud, the secretary, and a manicurist who prepared to sit on a jump seat. Lucian had climbed up front. There came a loud SPLAT!!

The manicurist held up a whoopee cushion and made a face. Jubee frowned, and the woman prepared to do his nails. The secretary began popping bon-bons into Dud's mouth. "Would 'ou like me to read to 'ou from *Captain Billy's Whiz Bang*?" she enthused.

MUSICAL CHAIRS

Spiff sighed and closed his copy of "Dodsworth."

Jubee settled back and smiled in contentment. "You've got to admit I'm smart," he congratulated himself. "All this luxury is due to me."

Lucian was of a different opinion. "Aw, you're not so smart." He held up a coin. "It's all due to my *lucky quarter*."

"Lucky quarter my ass," said Jubee. He grabbed the coin and threw it out the window.

"Waa-aaa-aaa!" cried his little brother. "That was a *new* quarter. Mommy gave it to me on my *third* birthday."

Even without a computer, Jubee could figure. "Runt is *five* years old. Two years ago runt was *three* years old. Nineteen ninety-one less two is 1989. STOP THE CAR!!! WE'VE GOT TO GET THAT QUARTER!"

They were in a wholesale area. The coin was bouncing down the street. The boys tumbled out and took off after it.

Down the street two elegantly tattered hoboes named Alphonse and Gaston were sitting on a nearby wall, their belongings in a kerchief by their side. Their eyes lit up at the sound of approaching money, and they saw the coin turn slightly and come to a rest under one of six new wooden chairs lined up back to back on the sidewalk. They looked at each other in satisfaction at the unexpected windfall and slid down from the wall.

The boys came to a halt a few feet from the chairs. They eyed the hoboes warily, and were in turn stared at in disbelief by the two men. Could these pint-sized J.P. Morgans in such expensive regalia really be after a *quarter*? Caution was the order of the day.

Suddenly there came a nearby woman's voice. "Now, Amaryllis, try it once again." It came from a nearby front apartment which had a "Piano Given" sign in its window. The music for "While Strolling in the Park One Day" began, and it gave the kids an idea. They placed their hands behind their backs and, whistling and skipping to the music, began to circle the chairs. With exaggerated finesse, the hoboes joined them.

THE WONDERFUL EDISON TIME MACHINE

The boys tipped their hats, and the hoboes reciprocated. The last boy and the first hobo twirled each other around and bowed with a deep flourish. A workman entered and carried a chair away. The music momentarily stopped on a sour note, and the participants rushed for the five chairs. Jubee was "out" and retired to the sidelines.

To the chorus of the song, the participants began again. By the end of the second bar, the workman removed another chair. When the music lesson again paused, there was another rush for the remaining seats. Only four were left, and this time Dud was out. The remaining strollers then started again; another chair was removed, and this time the fat hobo was out. He joined the bystanders.

Now only *two* chairs remained. Spiff, Lucian and the thin hobo circled them, still whistling. The workman then returned and took *both* chairs. The quarter was revealed. All three dove for it. Spiff was knocked aside and the hobo got it. He took off running, with Lucian in fast pursuit.

MUSICAL CHAIRS

There was a wagonload of empty wooden barrels near a loading dock, and the hobo made to hide in one. Lucian jumped in after him, and the ensuing melee caused the wagon to begin to roll downhill. It was soon scattering barrels as it gained momentum.

Further down the slope was McFarlan Park with a large flagpole and a sign which read "Flint's own mayor, the Honorable William H. McKeighan, going for the Flagpole Sitting Record — 115 days." The careening wagon was headed directly for the pole.

Atop it was a small platform with a pup tent, a bugle, a bucket on a pull-rope, a beaded floor lamp, and a glass-enclosed stock ticker. Mayor McKeighan, dressed in a cutaway coat and a top hat, sat in a rocking chair reading "The Wall Street Journal."

Someone cried, *"There's going to be a crash!"*

Mayor McKeighan leaped to the stock ticker. There was a loud crash, and the mayor had a sickly look as there came the sound of a rapidly rising vibration.

The wagon had come to an abrupt stop at the bottom of the pole. The hobo extracted himself from the broken barrel and started to run. Immediately the mayor landed on him. Lucian took the quarter from the unconscious hobo's hand just before spectators rushed up.

*   *   *   *   *

That evening Jubee and Margaret were walking on the beach. They passed Mr. Gatsby, who was looking across the lake with a handheld telescope. Margaret was the first to speak.

"Did you hear Mayor McKeighan fell off his flagpole?"

"He should be more careful," the boy replied.

Margaret suddenly stopped. "I wish you'd tell me where you live. I want to come *see you*."

"I *told* you. Someplace where they don't allow women."

"Where's that?"

THE WONDERFUL EDISON TIME MACHINE

Jubee was wise beyond his years. "If men told women where they couldn't go, they'd go there."

Margaret persisted. "You told me your parents died years before you were born, so you don't live at home. The vice squad closed Flint's only monastery, so you don't live there. I *thought* of trying the YMCA, but with *your* money…I KNOW! You live at the *Millionaires Club*."

Jubee was suspicious. "They don't allow women there?"

"No."

"Then that's where I live. Third floor back."

Margaret resumed walking. "Well, I can still visit you in the lobby."

Jubee gulped. "You can?"

"Sure," Margaret said. "I'll come over sometime this week. I've a new frock I want to show you."

"Aw hell," the boy said. He felt tricked.

Margaret was on him like a wildcat. "JUBEE METZENBAUM! You said a *bad word* in front of me. You don't care for me at all."

The boy was humbled. "You should hear how the girls talk at Cen-"

Margaret started to cry. "So you *do* know other girls."

"Holy cow," thought Jubee. He took her in his arms. "I'm sorry. And I *do* want to see your new frock. I'm sure it's better than the other two thousand you've shown me."

And they continued on.

CHAPTER SEVENTEEN

THE DOG THAT HATED
DEMOCRATS

At one time in the city of Flint there had been a home for indigent Indian children, but as the town progressed, the land became more valuable. So one winter the building was torn down and its occupants transferred by sled to a kraal in Kalamazoo. Some of them actually got there.

In its place there rose a splendid structure of marble, mahogany and gold relief, the envy of any Medici who happened by. Its hushed hallways, elegant suites and sculptured stairways offered welcome sanctuary from the lesser, unwashed denizens of Genesee County, not to mention harping wives of fashion and frivolity. This bastion of male conservativism was known as the Millionaires Club, and its large bronze plaque in front grandly informed anyone who could read Latin that it had been established in 1872.

It was before this edifice on Court Street that the four boys stood just two days later. The chauffeur had helped them disembark, and they all struggled with a variety of musical instruments and luggage with money sticking out.

Several cows in Scotland had sacrificed themselves for the "Dun & Bradstreet" briefcase Jubee carried. Dud's, no less imposing, read "Booz•Allen & Hamilton," a firm he'd never heard of. Spiff wielded an accumulation of "Forbes" magazines and a book entitled "How Now, Dow?" Lucian hefted two large accounting ledgers and directed at them his usual indelicate verbiage.

With a camaraderie born of confidence and currency, the boys entered the elaborate foyer. Ahead of them was a reception desk and a preoccupied concierge. They set their belongings down, and the three older ones continued on to peer into the lounge.

It was a richly-paneled room with leather armchairs, each containing an elderly slumbering millionaire. Most of their faces were covered with newspaper financial sections. A few members were frozen at small tables over eternal chess games. The clock on the mantel, a gift from President McKinley, had been trained not to tick above a whisper. There was an Al Smith dartboard on the wall, and a Great Dane snoozing on a throw rug. The kids looked on in awe.

Suddenly there was a commotion behind them. A gentleman was at the desk, frothing at the mouth.

"I *demand* to know why my application to join the Millionaires Club has been denied. I *have* a million dollars. I have *more* than a million dollars."

"I'm sorry, sir," the concierge said, "but the club rules state that if you're not a Republican, you didn't come by the money honestly."

"POPPYCOCK!" the man cried. "I *am* a Republican. And I'll punch any man who says I'm not."

The concierge was adamant. "We realize your application *says* you're a Republican, but Thaddeus feels you're not."

"Show me this Thaddeus who's calling me a liar," thundered the man. "Where is the lout?"

The concierge pointed. "Right over there." The Great Dane was in the doorway, teeth bared for attack.

The gentleman was incredulous. "You mean I was turned down by a *dog*?"

"Not just *any* dog," the concierge replied. "Thaddeus has been here ever since 1917, when he bit some Wobbly strikers and almost died of rabies."

"But a dog can't tell the difference between a Democrat and a Republican."

"This one can. It's a combination of things. Democrats don't eat rich foods like caviar and lobster thermidor. Democrats use inferior grades of soap, and purchase their clothing off the rack. Democrats even walk subserviently,

THE DOG THAT HATED DEMOCRATS

not in broad strides like the titans of finance. And their handwriting is small and cramped, like they have something to conceal. Believe me, the dog can tell. Here, I'll *show* you."

The concierge whistled and the dog came loping over. He examined the application, then barked furiously. He lunged at the man, who immediately fled, and within moments agonized cries came from outside. The dog then re-entered with part of the man's pants in his teeth. He passed the boys in triumph and resumed his position on the rug.

The boys watched in consternation. Jubee looked inquiringly at Dud. The boy admitted, sheepishly, "My dad was a Stevenson Democrat."

Jubee frowned and turned to Spiff. Spiff unhappily turned back the lapel of his jacket, revealing a Dukakis button. Jubee then looked at Lucian. The little boy blew up an "I partied with Ted Kennedy in Palm Beach" balloon. Jubee was dismayed.

Then he saw a black woman dropping laundry down a chute, and he got an idea. He whispered to the chauffeur, who promptly left, and then to his friends.

The kids grabbed their musical instruments and began playing the 1920s song "Crazy Words, Crazy Tune." The music proved so catching the concierge came from behind the counter and joined in. The boys began to sing the words, and when "black bottom" came up, Spiff, who actually had one, made to "moon" the group. But Jubee held his pants up, thereby avoiding an X rating for any movie made out of this story.

At the chorus the concierge did the stanza on Napoleon and Washington, then Spiff the third on Simon Legree. Jubee changed the last lines to, "And in the White House the other day, what did our President George Bush say?" and they all responded with "Vo-do-de-o-vo-do-do-do-o-do."

Jubee and Dud had danced unnoticed out of view. To the music they carried a surprised Thaddeus in his throw rug up to the laundry chute, where they deposited him. The dog slid down an incline into the basement, where the chauffeur awaited him with a large burlap bag.

Still keeping time to the music, the two boys re-entered the foyer. The song ended, and all the participants shook hands. The concierge then returned to his station, and the kids happily extended to him their applications for membership.

CHAPTER EIGHTEEN

AWASH IN LIBERALISM

One week later nothing had changed in the lounge of the Millionaires Club except that the kids had taken up residence. A butler was pouring a club member a martini from a cocktail shaker. Spiff and Dud were playing mah jongg. Jubee was attempting to read a newspaper, but the quiet was so funereal it was making him nervous.

Dud noticed, and informed him, "It was *your* idea to move in here."

"Shut up," said Jubee. "Here come our drinks."

A butler appeared with a tray holding a cocktail shaker and three frosted glasses. He shook the silver container, then poured out a milkshake. Just then there came the sound of a police siren and a screeching of tires.

Lucian dashed in the foyer, looked frantically about, and then ran off. A moment later cops stormed in.

Spiff accused Dud angrily. "I thought *you* were watching him."

"He can untie every knot I know," said Dud.

The kids huddled down as the cops indicated with their hands they were looking for a pint-sized individual. The concierge shook his head. The cops then ambled into the lounge. Their eyes lit up at a shaking newspaper, and they noisily snatched it away. Revealed was a cadaverous man whose trembling hands were still extended. All the club members angrily went "Sh-h-h-h-h," and the disgusted policemen left the room.

Spiff sighed. "Too bad school's out. We could put Lucian in kindergarten."

THE WONDERFUL EDISON TIME MACHINE

Jubee had returned to reading the newspaper. "Say," he said excitedly. "Not *all* the schools are out. RING JENKINS FOR THE CAR!"

* * * * *

The Montahooey School was a private progressive institution located out near Mt. Morris. Its graduates were sought in all forty-eight states, and bulletins regarding their activities and whereabouts were broadcast almost daily. It was rumored that the government planned to house the most notable of them in a new facility in San Francisco Bay, and the school had already instituted a crash course on the behavior of tides.

The next day Jubee and Spiff were listening reverently to its founder, Dr. John Hooey, who was happily pontificating in his office while Dud unwound Lucian from the stout ropes that enveloped him.

"In the Montahooey School, and using the Montahooey methods (which *I* personally developed), nothing will prevent your little brother from doing anything he wants."

"Nothing prevents him now," said Dud.

"But *do* go on," said Spiff and Jubee.

"Our goal is to free the naturally inquisitive libido from the rigidity and repression of modern conventionality," the learned pedagogue continued.

"Oh, yes," agreed Spiff and Jubee. "Less rigidity."

Dud grabbed Lucian as the lad attempted to bolt. "Just *take* him," he said.

Dr. Hooey led the way into a classroom. "Here we place no restrictions on the imagination," he explained. He stopped by a table where an impossible boy was testing a moveable metal gate in a papier-mâché mountain pass, below which lay the houses of a village.

"Young master Nixon is building a water gate."

"It's going to flood *all* the people down below," the youth said with relish. "They won't kick *me* around."

Dr. Hooey continued on. "We feel the Polanski boy over there may

someday rival Michelangelo." A leering lad was copying in clay the undraped form of a little girl. Just beyond, another boy with a changing face was pouring chemicals from one beaker to another.

Dr. Hooey pointed to a corner. "That's Bonnie Parker's little girl over there. She's made friends with Malcolm X." The two children were firing machine guns at a moving target. Lucian ran over to join them.

The good doctor backed up suddenly as four girls in Red Cross caps rushed past him carrying a stretcher containing a bandaged boy connected to some plasma. "And here they're playing Nurse Edith Cavell," he said.

The educator then stopped by a well-stocked bar and accepted a highball from a round-faced lad holding a copy of "Dr. Hooey's Guide to the Bar," complete with an engraved cover of a tipsy Goddess of Justice. He tasted the drink.

"That's a lot better, Jackie," he said, and the boy beamed back, "HOW SWEET IT IS."

The group was outside now, shaking hands. Behind them the four nurses were helping *real* medics place their patient in a *real* ambulance. It departed with siren blaring.

THE WONDERFUL EDISON TIME MACHINE

"Your brother can be available to you on weekends," the doctor smiled.

"Weekends we're away," said Jubee hastily, and the three of them made tracks for the car. Safely inside they called back gaily, "Don't get him mad or he'll eat grass." "Keep him locked up during full moons." The car sped off as Dr. Hooey waved goodbye.

*   *   *   *   *

"No more worries," the kids said a few moments later as the Rolls careened down a deserted street. "We're free." "It's clear sailing from here on." They settled back in its rich upholstery and did not notice they were passing a ramshackle warehouse with a faded sign: "Krockashita and Sons — Secondhand Junk." A forlorn wagon sat in front.

CHAPTER NINETEEN

LAND OF CHERRY
LAND OF SNOW

The Krockashita warehouse was actually a highly secret automotive laboratory whose location was known only to a select few thousand of the most observant burghers in the city of Flint. Messages coded in Aramaic to Swahili arrived there daily, most of them with postage due, and the three industrial spies often worked into the wee small hours of the night attempting to decipher them. The walls were festooned with blueprints, some from the time the Roman aqueducts were new, and there were lathes and presses in abundance.

On this auspicious day Gosoaka, Osocka and Unseemly were jubilantly toasting one another with glasses of steaming sake. They wore their official Krockashita Motors jackets, which featured a large embroidered earthenware jar, below which golden rays extended from the sea. Beside them was an easel with a map of the Japanese islands, a rising sun flag on one side, and a cherry tree and Mount Fujiyama on the other. Each man grabbed a pointer, and they broke into the company chant.

Osocka indicated the rising sun. "KROCKASHITA HITS THE SPOT."

Gosoaka indicated the mainland. "FOUR MAIN ISLANDS, THAT'S A LOT."

Unseemly indicated the cherry tree and Mount Fujiyama. "LAND OF CHERRY, LAND OF SNOW."

Then all of them in unison: "THAT WE FEEL IS *WAY TO GO!*"

The spies then broke into cheerleader contortions as the three canisters entered and scurried in excitement. Osocka silenced the others with a cut of

THE WONDERFUL EDISON TIME MACHINE

his hand. He took a one-stringed musical instrument and plunked a note. Immediately the men broke into a woeful dirge that sounded like three cats dying. The canisters stood at attention and, mercifully, the song was short.

Unseemly took a folded piece of cloth and reverently extended it to Gosoaka, who bowed in turn and presented it to his father. Osocka bowed in gratitude, then glanced to his left.

An oversized car, a nightmare of conflicting parts, was slumbering nearby. Its radiator had a menacing grin, and its cap was a sumo wrestler. A flagpole aerial was on its side, and its headlamp eyes were closed. The vehicle was chugging lightly, as if snoring.

Osocka frowned and, bowing, handed the cloth back to Gosoaka, who handed it back to Unseemly. The hapless youth had been chosen.

He gulped and warily approached the car. It remained asleep. He looked back, and the others shooed him on. Gingerly he unfolded the cloth. It was a rising sun flag.

The car opened one headlamp. It snorted. It opened its other headlamp.

It snorted again. Apparently it did not like the flag. Its grillwork turned to teeth, and with a roar it charged.

Unseemly had no choice but to use the flag like a matador's cape. The car flashed by him, skidded, and turned again. Gosoaka and Osocka ran for their lives, followed by the canisters. The car charged again, and to the music of the bull ring, Unseemly adroitly avoided it. The car swerved and crashed into shop equipment. Gosoaka's and Osocka's heads popped up from nearby rice baskets. The car regrouped, and Unseemly dropped the flag and fled. It pursued him vengefully, its headlamps red with rage, and when it finally stopped, the laboratory had been destroyed.

Three rice baskets now contained the Krockashitas, who cautiously rose and looked about. They spotted the car sucking water at a water cooler. Osocka waved his beard and bleated like a goat. His sons mashed him back into his basket and grinned apologetically. Unforgiving, the car charged with a final roar. The canisters were petrified with fright. Each basket sprouted legs and ran in circles of confusion. At the last moment they jumped aside, and the car crashed through the wall.

The car emerged in a shower of bricks onto Industrial Avenue and fired down the street. It stopped at the corner. Growling and meshing its gears, it heard the sound of circus music. To its left was the tail end of a circus parade. The car drove slowly down the street and joined it. It smiled and replaced its sumo radiator cap with one of Uncle Sam. It ran up an American flag on its aerial and began playing a calliope rendition of "The Star Spangled Banner." Kids rushed over to befriend it, and the car moved off, happy in its newfound home.

CHAPTER TWENTY

THE GATHERING STORM

Several days later, the experimental Wizzer Playboy was barreling down a country lane in a cloud of dust. Derby was at the wheel, and David in the passenger seat. The latter whooped enthusiastically over the roar of the engine and wrote some figures in a notebook.

Derby grinned and turned a lever on the dashboard. The car reined in its massive power and began to purr. It reduced to a respectable speed and approached a long, high hedge. Spiff and Dud darted out and pivoted an opening to let the car through. It skirted the George Willoughby mansion by driving on the lawn, and headed toward the greenhouse. Meddlesome noted the car's return and picked up a telephone.

Jubee, Margaret and Meadowcroft greeted the car as it came to a halt, and were joined by Spiff and Dud. The two mechanics got out, tired but happy.

"It worked just fine this time," David cried, brushing back his wind-blown hair. "No trouble, not even from the carburetors. All the bugs are now worked out."

Margaret felt the time was opportune to ask a favor. "Tonight's the opening of Pearl's Harbor Club. I haven't been to a party in ages, and Jubee wants to take me. Can we take the new Wizzer? We'll be ever so careful, and Derby can drive."

"Well, I can hardly say no, since Jubee's money is paying for all the retooling," her brother replied. "And Derby can fix anything that goes wrong.

THE GATHERING STORM

But once you get there be sure to cover it with canvas. So far we've been lucky. No one has gotten wind of our new model."

*　*　*　*　*

Meanwhile, at the Krockashita laboratory, the three spies sat forlornly amid the wreckage. Their dreams of glory had turned to dust. A few steps away, the canisters watched with sorrow. They huddled together; then one of them projected a grainy image of David saying, "…Otis and I have been working on a top-secret project, something we believe will revolutionize the automobile industry…come down to the greenhouse after supper." The Krockashitas stirred with hope at this new information, and the canisters rejoiced.

*　*　*　*　*

The never-ending party was, as usual, going strong, and no one thought it strange when four ill-mannered men dressed as revolutionaries entered. They were the people Meddlesome had phoned. They all had long black beards, and one of them carried a round bomb with a fuse.

Miss Swansdown Swoonsudden, a society matron, saw them and exclaimed, "Isn't that cute? They've come as anarchists." A second one chimed in, "They're just too, too divine." The men squeezed their breasts to the sound of a bicycle horn as they marched scowlingly by, appropriating food. The women giggled and each adjusted her décolletage.

*　*　*　*　*

Outside, the anarchists ran to the greenhouse, arriving just in time to see the new Wizzer Playboy recede into the distance. They slumped, dejected, then heard a noise and tiptoed to a nearby bush.

The canisters were on the other side in earnest confab. One of them was projecting an image of what had just transpired. Jubee was seen getting into the car. "You got the canvas packed?" Spiff's voice was audible: "All packed." "Okay, get the doors, Dud." He sat down beside Margaret as Spiff bounded in.

"Show Derby where to go," the girl said, and Jubee reached for something to make a sign. The canisters looked up and saw the anarchists. They stopped the projection and attempted to escape, but were quickly captured.

THE WONDERFUL EDISON TIME MACHINE

* * * * *

They were in a Kafka-esque interrogation room. A blinding light was on the canisters, who were on high stools, and they were close to tears. All of the anarchists were beardless now, and their discarded costumes were on a nearby chair. Their jumpsuits had the words "Ossified Motors — Big as a Dinosaur," and one of the men was operating on a canister from the back.

An electric spark shocked the center canister, and while the others looked on fearfully, it projected a scene of Yokohama Harbor. Not satisfied, the technician probed further, and in obvious pain, the canister projected a picture of the Emperor on horseback. Exasperated, one of the men brought up

a heavy-duty battery. The canisters wailed in consternation as it was attached to the center one.

There was a bright, bluish light, and the canister began flashing the Jubee car scene taken in the greenhouse. As soon as the sign "To Pearl's Harbor Club, Mr. Crewe" was seen, the men grabbed the round bomb and left. They didn't even wait to see Dud vault into the car, or the three boys shout "Yaba-daba-doo-oo!" as they moved off.

One of the canisters jumped down from its perch and peered outside the door. It motioned for the others to follow, and they filed out.

CHAPTER TWENTY-ONE

HI-JINKS AT THE HARBOR CLUB

The Harbor Club had been transformed by a flamboyant designer of questionable sexuality into a striking configuration of curves and chrome, all laid out in the severest geometric homage to the new Industrial Age. The floor was polished darkness and so mirrored the ceiling with its reflective ball of multi-colored sleet that it created the giddy impression of being trapped in a shower of stars. Fringed and beaded curtains shimmered everywhere, and there were elongated terra cotta statues in almost every alcove, lit eerily from below to enhance their aloof, unworldly features.

The entire effect was as if its creators had first undergone a fever-stricken trip to the Yucatan and then recuperated at a high-class bordello on the Riviera. It had the appearance and the efficiency of the inside of a machine, with its carefully coiffured customers the only moving parts. It was glass and plastic and zebra skins. It was clocks without numbers, and ice-cold polished metal. It was Art Deco at its highest, something new and strange to the staid inhabitants of Genesee County.

Opening night found a black musician playing a soulful saxophone, backed up by other musicians in snappy attire. There was a respectable number of blacks and whites in attendance, but they sat on opposite sides of the room and appeared to be uncomfortable. Cigarettes glowed dimly, and lazy swirls of smoke hung heavy in the stagnant air. Eyes were the only thing that moved.

THE WONDERFUL EDISON TIME MACHINE

Dressed to the nines, Pearl, Reverend Honeysuckle and several others were manning the doorway and greeting guests. A group of boisterous blacks entered. Pearl lifted the tails of several of their tuxedos and extracted flasks of liquor.

"Ain't no hooch allowed in here," she said, and the men continued meekly on. Suddenly her eyes lit up. Jubee, Dud, Spiff, Margaret and Derby were entering. Margaret looked particularly beautiful in her new evening dress. An attendant removed her wrap as the group was warmly welcomed.

"How's it going?" Jubee said.

"Well, the crowd's pretty good," Pearl replied, "but they're not livening up."

"Well, the evening's young," the youth replied. "Give 'em a chance."

He then advanced to the three bankers, who were awkwardly waiting with their wives. Dud spied the secretary just exiting the powder room with her friend, who had come along for Derby. Spiff inspected the house through a curtain. Reverend Honeysuckle quietly led Pearl aside.

"I see you didn't mention it to Jubee."

"About Slugsy? I don't want to worry him."

"Well, they say *Slugsy* is coming. After all this *was* his club."

Hi-Jinks at the Harbor Club

"Even Al Capone is afraid of *him*," said one of the others who had overheard. A second man chimed in: "They say he's a master of disguise."

"Calm down," said Pearl. "Nobody's ever seen Slugsy, so nobody knows *what* he looks like. Besides, he never leaves Detroit. Everything's going to be fine." She then looked at the doorway. "Uh-oh, I spoke too soon."

Six robed and hooded men were coming up the steps. "Don't mention the cover charge," she advised, preparing herself. "They're already covered."

"Hi!" said the lead robed man. "We're NUTS."

"I can see that," said Pearl.

The man pointed to his emblem, a large walnut. "**N**eighbors **U**pholding **T**otal **S**egregation. We're against race-mixing in Genesee County."

"Well, there sure ain't no race-mixin' here. Go see for yourself. AND HAVE SOME PUNCH."

"Maybe they're Slugsy's men in disguise," whispered Reverend Honeysuckle as the men continued on.

"Naw!" said Pearl, derisively. "They're just NUTS."

The hooded figures entered the club and seated themselves in the rear. A few white couples were now dancing.

Outside the club a black was standing guard. He heard a creaking sound and, rounding a corner, saw a horizontal basement entry. He opened one of its folding doors and descended the steps.

He bounced the beam from his flashlight around, then guided it along a bottom wall. Revealed was a small ornamental grate and a heavy barrel. The guard moved the barrel, and with a terrifying screech a cat sprang out. The guard looked around again, then left. The barrel now blocked the grate, and the grate was being rattled.

Inside the grate was a small passageway, and a figure hustled down its length. Within a few yards it came to an abrupt end. The figure groped a bit, then lit a match. Revealed was a hinged doorway with a knob, which the figure quickly turned.

The Wonderful Edison Time Machine

There was a room beyond, shrouded in gloom. The figure stepped out of the hidden doorway and stood unsteadily, feeling along the wall for a switch. It found one, and the flooding light revealed *Lucian*, wearing a Montahooey cap and sweater. He gaped at what he saw.

It was a snug and cozy gangster hideout. But everything was miniature: the furniture, the pictures on the wall, the bottles of liquor behind the bar — even the three machine guns aligned against a wall. Like a visitor to Aladdin's cave, the little boy wandered through the room and into the bedroom. The bed was covered with heart-shaped pillows, and above it was a portrait of a pint-sized woman with one foot on a car bumper and holding a machine gun. It was labeled "Mother." There was a floor-length mirror to the left, and a closet filled with miniature clothes. A gangster outfit had been laid out. It was exactly Lucian's size.

*   *   *   *   *

A short time later, the boy was dressed in the gangster outfit and was examining himself in the mirror. He then walked back into the living room, took a cigar from a humidor, and seeing some curved stairs at the end of the room, went over to mount them.

To loud sounds of music, Lucian climbed into a hidden space beside the hallway leading from the kitchen to the nightclub area. The front wall from four feet up was partially shuttered by long wooden slats. The back wall contained a mammoth selection of liquor bottles. Piercing the slatted wall was a circular revolving table. The outside portion contained three punch bowls filled with lemonade. Pearl and Reverend Honeysuckle came into view.

"This party will never loosen up as long as those NUTS are here," the woman said irately. "I wish we could get them drunk."

"It's too bad we're good Christians," consoled the Reverend.

Lucian pondered their predicament. He saw a wooden catch. He lifted it back and tested the table. It moved. He turned it counterclockwise and the three punch bowls, each containing a block of ice, swung into view. The lad then stepped to the bar and began taking down bottles. From his back pocket he pulled out a copy of "Dr. Hooey's Guide to the Bar."

*　*　*　*　*

There was a deeply rutted road out near the Harbor Club. Its headlights off, a limousine had drawn up. From it came a raspy voice.

"You mugs stay here."

The back door opened. First came a spinning yo-yo, then spats. Then a diminutive man who snarled as he negotiated the treacherous height of the running board. He adjusted his tie and cruelly challenged the sky in open mockery. It was *Slugsy* himself. And he was the spitting image of Lucian.

*　*　*　*　*

Back inside the club, Lucian was smoking the cigar and emptying liquor into a bowl. He swung the table around, revealing three new empty ones. Discarded bottles were in abundance, plus a tubful of ice he had removed. The party sounded more lively now.

*　*　*　*　*

The guard was standing by the basement entrance. Slugsy rounded the corner of the building, smoking a cigar and wearing a homburg.

"Hey, little boy," the guard admonished, "you shouldn't smoke." Slugsy beckoned the guard to stoop down. There was a resounding THWACK that startled sleeping birds. The guard was sprawled out cold. The gangster removed his brass knuckles and lifted a folding door.

THE WONDERFUL EDISON TIME MACHINE

Moments later, Slugsy stepped into his secret hideaway. He looked around suspiciously, then headed for the bedroom. He swung back the picture of his mother and removed a small ledger from a wall safe. He flipped through its pages, then snarled in relief.

Upstairs, Lucian noticed his cigar had gone out, so he retreated down the steps to get another.

Slugsy dried his hands and threw the towel back into the bathroom. He headed toward a small table that held his hat and ledger.

Lucian re-entered the room and walked by the doorway just as Slugsy did. They both thought it was the mirror and stopped to spruce up. With identical movements, each was unaware it was the other. Both took combs from their back pockets and combed their hair. Both put fingers in their mouths to inspect their teeth, and both admired their profiles. Satisfied with their handsomeness, they continued on.

Lucian took a cigar from the humidor, then stopped to consider what he'd seen. He returned and extended his head into the doorway just as Slugsy did.

Lucian's face was one of wide-eyed innocence compared to the malevolent countenance of the Detroit gangster. Both retracted their heads, then put them back again. Something was wrong.

They both jumped across the opening, then skipped back in perfect unison. They picked up imaginary machine guns and sprayed each other. Slugsy looked at the smugly-satisfied Lucian. Both had cigars in their mouths. Grinning evilly, Slugsy *lit* his. Lucian did the same, then blew smoke in the gangster's face.

Stymied, Slugsy took out his yo-yo, Lucian doing likewise. He performed a simple trick; the lad imitated it. He tried a more elaborate trick, and it was duck soup to the boy. Lucian then initiated his own yo-yo trick and ended with a "Ta-da!" stance. The gangster failed to duplicate it.

Lucian's smile of triumph quickly turned to shock as Slugsy raised a

JUBEE AND MARGARET WERE STARTLED TO SEE LUCIAN IN THE DOORWAY,
WITH SLUGSY GIVING CHASE.

revolver to his face. In panic, the little boy did the same. The guns were barrel to barrel. Slugsy cocked his, but Lucian fired first — a squirt gun. The gangster recoiled, and Lucian ran off. Slugsy grabbed his hat and ledger and took off after him.

Moments later, Lucian emerged in the shuttered room and exited through a hidden door. He disappeared down the outside hallway only seconds before Slugsy appeared.

Margaret and Jubee were seated at a nightclub table. The girl had barely touched her lemonade, but the boy had downed a quantity.

"Don't you like your lemonade?" he inquired, his speech a little slurred.

"It's making me feel dizzy," she replied.

Jubee then saw Lucian in one doorway and Slugsy in another.

"Well, it's making *me* see double!" he said.

Jubee stumbled to his feet as Slugsy renewed the chase. Lucian ran down a hall towards the men's room.

Inside the lavatory the black guard, his head in bandages and his left arm in a sling, was being attended by a doctor.

"It was *ten* guys, I tell you, big as barns," he cried. "I didn't have a chance."

Lucian rushed in and entered the nearest stall, snapping the lock behind him.

The guard went into convulsions. "THAT'S HIM. *That's the guy who beat me up.*"

Lucian unsnapped the lock and looked out, a picture of innocence.

The guard leaped up. "*Don't let him hit me again*," he cried, and rushed out, only to immediately collide with a waiter carrying food. Both fell down as Slugsy skidded up. Jubee entered also, just as the guard saw the gangster.

"THAT'S HIM!" the guard cried anew. "*That's the guy who beat me up.*"

The doctor indicated he felt the man was crazy, and several helpers led the sobbing guard away. Slugsy looked around and snarled at the woodwork. Jubee had reached his limit.

THE WONDERFUL EDISON TIME MACHINE

"So," he addressed the gangster. "Up to your old tricks, you party crasher. And *smoking*, too."

Slugsy noticed him for the first time. "Say, listen, you two-bit punk," he growled.

"And don't give me your Cagney imitation," Jubee said, forcing the gangster's homburg down over his face.

Slugsy struggled frantically. "Lemme go, lemme go. Who turned out the lights?"

Jubee thrust the gangster through the lavatory door. Inside, Lucian crouched down within the stall. Slugsy, still blinded, pulled out a revolver and waved it wildly.

Jubee stood firm. "It isn't nice to point guns at people, even if it *is* only a squirt gun. Someday you might have a *real* one." He snatched it from Slugsy and threw it in a waste container, where it went off with a bang and made a hole. The boy jumped back in astonishment, then spoke again forcefully.

"So you think you're tough, huh?"

He turned the gangster upside down, and a dagger, brass knuckles, a hypodermic syringe and a hand grenade fell to the ground.

"What *are* they teaching you at that school?" he frowned. "Well, here comes the final lesson of the day."

With that, he turned Slugsy over his knee and, using the ledger from the gangster's back pocket, gave him a good spanking. The gangster left bawling. Jubee then scooped up the paraphernalia on the floor and dumped it in the trash. After he left, Lucian flushed the toilet, just to be on the safe side.

* * * * *

Outside, Slugsy climbed the rise to where his bodyguards awaited. The chauffeur was always the most articulate. "Gee, boss. Did ya find da book?"

Slugsy pulled himself into the limousine and sat down carefully. "Shut up and throw me your cushion," he rasped as the car was started.

* * * * *

Back in the shuttered room, Lucian happily returned to pouring alcohol.

* * * * *

The crowd was more animated now at the Harbor Club. Spirited music was being played. First the blacks would dance, and then the whites, including Margaret and Jubee, who were just returning to their table.

"No, really!" Margaret was saying. "I'm having a wonderful time. But tomorrow night is Epworth League."

Jubee was bleary. "What's that?"

Margaret: "Our Methodist Church youth group."

"I'm a member of Zealots for Zionism," he volunteered.

Margaret: "What's that?

"Right now I have no idea," he slurred, looking around the room. They both got up to go.

Outside, Jubee and Margaret descended the steps as the family car drove up. When the girl was safely inside, Jubee closed the door, then leaned against it. Margaret gave him a kiss, and as the car moved off the boy fell back.

"And *away she goes*." He waved with a sweep, then unsteadily walked back up the steps.

Had his eyes been able to focus, he might have seen four men who were skirting several parked automobiles and approaching a car covered with canvas. Looking around carefully, one of them pulled back the cover, revealing the resplendent new Wizzer. Another lifted the hood, while a third opened a round bomb containing sticks of dynamite and an alarm clock. The fourth one set the mechanism. "Eight-thirty should do fine," he said.

They placed the bomb deep within the engine compartment, replaced the hood and canvas, and quickly disappeared.

Re-entering the club, Jubee saw Spiff counting the receipts. Derby was in a silent conversation with his date, who looked at him adoringly. The bankers were in a high stakes poker game with some prosperous-looking blacks, while the three sets of wives, high as kites, were shrieking in the background. The party was very noisy now. Jubee found the punch bowl empty, then was astonished when a full one appeared. He helped himself to a generous portion, and then stepped over two bodies, which proved to be Dud and the secretary, locked in an embrace.

"Sure beats the prom at Central High," said Dud, looking up.

Listing like he'd struck an iceberg, Jubee entered the main room. It was a scene of wild abandon. People were frantically dancing with no regard for decorum, age or race. Many were dancing on the tabletops, while others made shameless love beneath them. Clothes were scattered in confusion, and the din was dreadful. So rampant was the sin it would have taken a month of Sundays for all the churches in Flint to repair the damage, assuming they would have even tried.

Jubee clutched a curtain as Pearl staggered by.

"What happened to the robed guys?" he inquired.

"The who…?" said Pearl.

"The…" Then he saw the NUTS, in advanced stages of intoxication, burst onto the floor. With hoods gone, they formed a line, bumping and grinding as they went. Reaching the bandstand, one of them grabbed some drumsticks and beat out a torrid solo, to the amazement of the musicians. They renewed their efforts, and the other NUTS joined in. They soon had sweethearts of both races perched upon their knees.

HI-JINKS AT THE HARBOR CLUB

Suddenly the Grand Pistachio, leader of all the NUTS, entered the room in full regalia.

"FENWICK! SMEDLEY!" he shouted. "WHAT IS THE MEANING OF THIS?"

The NUTS grabbed the Grand Pistachio and threw him out an open window. There came a resounding splash, and they resumed their playing and their lovemaking as the party intensified.

Outside, a few people straggled to their cars and drove off into the night as the club rocked with a fervor that could have been heard as far away as Windsor, had not its inhabitants long since been tucked into their trundle beds and fallen fast asleep.

CHAPTER TWENTY-TWO

THE DAY OF INFAMY

Dawn came, and the sun rose slowly over the lake. It was Sunday, August 4, 1929, a day which would live in infamy.

The remnants of the Grand Pistachio's costume was floating by the shore. In the canvas-covered Wizzer, ticking could be heard. In the interior of Pearl's Harbor Club, the clock read 7:35. The room was semi-dark, and Spiff, Dud, Jubee and Lucian were arranged in various piles, deep in sleep among the debris.

Derby was out in a rowboat on the lake, fishing. Behind him a periscope rose and observed him. The mute sensed something and turned around, but the periscope had disappeared. He resumed fishing, and when he looked up again, an entire Japanese submarine had surfaced and the three Krockashitas were rapidly paddling towards shore. Derby began rowing furiously for the beach. Upon landing, the spies headed for the parking lot, and the young man for the club.

Once inside, Derby dodged overturned tables and chairs as he rushed to the window. He pulled a distorted Venetian blind, and the morning sun fell upon the sleeping boys like rays from a Japanese flag. He then grabbed a large drum and marched around the room beating it. The kids began to stir.

"What is it?" "Shut up." "What a night!" Their eyes were still half-closed.

Derby rushed to the xylophone and began beating out the first stanza of "The Japanese Sandman." He then performed a brief, mechanical walk with a toothy grin, and bowed in imitation of the Krockashitas. The kids began to sit up.

"What's he want?" "What's he trying to say?"

The mute charged behind a counter and re-emerged with a pickle crock. He ran to a nearby "Restrooms" sign and pointed to the crock, then the sign. There was a boom in the distance.

"THE KROCKASHITAS!" cried the kids in unison.

There was a terrific blast, and the letters CLUB came crashing through the roof into the room.

Out on the submarine, Japanese Navy personnel were loading another shell into an artillery gun, while others jumped into a pontoon. Jubee and Dud looked out the window, then ran around in circles.

"What'll we do? WHAT'LL WE DO?"

Derby noiselessly yelled "Help" into a phone receiver. Spiff grabbed it. *"The line's been cut."* There was another boom.

It was a direct hit on the roof-line of the club. The "S" fell back in smoke, and the sign now read PEARL HARBOR.

The navy boat with armed men was fast approaching shore. The kids again looked out the window.

"Holy shit; they're *invading*. It's every man for himself."

In panic, they ran out of the room, passing Lucian, who was now dressed as an army colonel and calmly clipping ammunition into three small machine guns. Sheepishly the boys filed back in and Lucian handed each a gun, indicating how to use it. The weapons were accepted gravely, although Jubee, noting Lucian, could not help but wonder: "Where *does* he get the costumes?"

With whoops, the boys bounded across the room and out onto the sun deck. The boat had landed, and sailors were leaping out. The boys began firing furiously.

"Eat lead! Back to Nipponland, you bastards," cried Dud and Jubee. On the beach, several sailors returned the fire.

Spiff aimed his weapon as bullets whizzed by. "This is the Flint *I* remember," he cried happily.

THE WONDERFUL EDISON TIME MACHINE

Faced with the overwhelming fire, the sailors retreated and began to paddle off. The three boys swaggered back into the room and put their weapons down. Jubee was ecstatic.

"That's the way Errol Flynn did it in 'Objective Burma.'"

"John Wayne did it even better in 'Sands of Iwo Jima,'" Dud exclaimed.

"How did a Japanese submarine get in Devil's Lake?" asked the more practical Spiff.

Jubee was admiring himself in a mirror. "Almost all the lakes around here have underwater outlets to Lake Erie."

"Yes," said Spiff, "but how did it get into *Lake Erie*? The St. Lawrence Seaway hasn't been built yet."

"Maybe it came in the Erie Canal," volunteered Dud.

"No, it's too shallow," rejoined Spiff.

Jubee was irritated. "Look, do we have to argue this now?"

His words were immediately drowned out as the sounds of a massive air armada filled the room. The boys again rushed to the windows. Lucian was already looking out through camouflaged binoculars.

"*This* was never in 'Sands of Iwo Jima,'" despaired Dud.

Ten Japanese biplanes were swooping in for the kill. Their pilots looked woodenly determined.

"What'll we do? WHAT'LL WE DO?" Again, they ran around in circles. Lucian walked up to them with flyswatters.

"Flyswatters!" the kids said flatly.

Stoically, they accepted the flyswatters and filed out onto the porch. They looked up into the sky. The first three biplanes were breaking formation and thundering down with machine guns blazing.

The boys assumed a fighting position, flyswatters to the front. The first plane entered. It was a miniature, some ten inches long. They quickly smashed it down, but the other two planes shot at them as they pulled away, causing the boys to hop around, holding their behinds.

WAVE AFTER WAVE OF PLANES SWEPT IN, AND THE BOYS FOUGHT VALIANTLY.

THE DAY OF INFAMY

Out on the submarine deck, six more miniature planes were being wound and set off.

It was a battle royal. Wave after wave of planes swept in, and the deck was littered with their wreckage. The boys fought valiantly and howled as they were hit again in the rear. But more formations droned in, and it was apparent they were being overwhelmed.

Lucian ran out with gas masks, pushing a large wheeled can of insect repellant. Jubee immediately grabbed it. Spiff was alarmed.

"Chemical warfare? What about the Geneva Convention?"

"Our country never signed it," Jubee shouted, laying down a thick, green stream of insect repellant. The planes were soon coughing and choking and sputtering to the deck, where the boys finished them off with renewed blows from the flyswatters. When the smoke cleared, it was plain they were victorious, but their euphoria was stillborn as they saw the Krockashitas pushing the canvas-covered Wizzer onto the submarine.

"THEY'RE STEALING THE WIZZER!" Jubee and Dud cried, and rushed out.

The three older boys raced through the parking lot with their machine guns. Derby was lying face-down on the pavement, a bloody pipe wrench nearby. Spiff stopped to help him as Lucian emerged from the club dressed as a Red Cross medic and carrying a first-aid kit.

Out on the submarine, with a final push the car went down a special hatch. The Krockashitas stood proudly on the deck. On a nearby bluff, the canisters were bouncing up and down in glee. Dud and Jubee were almost to the beach.

Captain Tsunami was in the conning tower, about to close its lid. The Krockashitas were making imploring gestures to go along. The captain shook his head and pointed to their legs. They were soaked with sand and water. The submarine began to submerge as the Krockashitas stood rigidly at attention and sang their mournful dirge.

On the embankment, the canisters were thunderstruck. They slid down the bluff, tumbled into the water, and swam out to save the Krockashitas, who clung to their backs as they returned to shore.

Nearby, the boys had reached the beach. The submarine was gone. In the Harbor Club, the minute hand of the wall clock lurched to 8:30.

Instantly, the surface of Devil's Lake exploded, flinging water and metal high into the air. Jubee and Dud fell back, then looked sadly at the scene. When the lake was again placid, they turned to go.

Back in the parking lot, they found Spiff ministering to Derby, who was still unconscious. A solemn Lucian came up, dressed as an undertaker and wearing a stovepipe hat. He placed a single lily in Derby's hand, and began to measure the body.

The mute opened his eyes and feebly sat up. The boys helped him to his feet.

"Sorry," said Jubee to his disappointed brother. "He's going to live."

CHAPTER TWENTY-THREE

AN IMPORTANT DISCOVERY

A few hours later, the three boys, David and Mr. Meadowcroft were exiting a hospital room.

"It's just a simple knock on the head," said David.

"He'll be okay," reassured Meadowcroft.

"We were dumb to take the car," said Jubee.

"We can build it again," said David. "And this time we'll keep it under guard."

Meadowcroft was not so sure. "The New York Auto Show is coming fast. Can we rebuild the car in three months?"

"We'll work day *and* night," said David. "We have that extra engine, and all the jigs and fixtures. We can do it. So long, boys."

The boys said goodbye and went to retrieve their jackets. A book fell out of Jubee's, and Dud picked it up. "What's this?" he asked.

"Oh, it's some schoolbook Lucifer had with him," his friend replied. "It probably shows sixty-nine ways Dick and Jane make love."

Dud briefly perused the book and then exclaimed, "It's better than that! Look, it belongs to Slugsy. His bookplate's in the front. It shows him standing on a pile of bodies."

Spiff grabbed the book and immediately marveled, "And he's *the spitting image of Lucifer.*"

Jubee was aghast. "That means…IT WAS SLUGSY I SPANKED." He fainted to the floor. Dud shouted down the hallway, "Is there a doctor in the house?"

THE WONDERFUL EDISON TIME MACHINE

A few moments later, several interns were administering to Jubee, while Spiff rapidly turned pages in the book. "Thanks, boys," said Jubee groggily. "Put it on my Visa card." The interns left, and the boy regained his feet.

Spiff's eyes were big, and he spoke in fear as he indicated the book.

"It's a record of all of Slugsy's rackets in Flint: his gambling joints and speakeasies, his bootleggers and trigger men; even where to leave payoffs for the police and get the best grades of cement."

Dud grabbed the book. "Not to mention monies owed for bootleg gin right up to *Rabbi Lupo of Beth Israel*." Jubee snatched the book from him. "And, he said, pointing, "*Bishop O'Malley of St. Matthew's*. It's a *joint* account."

A map dropped out. Spiff picked it up and examined it.

"Look, a fold-out map. It shows how they get the liquor in. See, down from Canada, across Lake Huron, then by touring cars to *Thread Lake*…then across the lake to…3923 Lakewood Court."

The boys looked up in stunned alarm. "*That's where Margaret lives!*"

CHAPTER TWENTY-FOUR

FORTS AND FANTASIES

It was now late afternoon. The three boys warily walked up the walled approach to the garage area of the George Willoughby mansion. In the distance, the Never-Ending Party was gearing up for another night of nihilism. Ahead of them were two heavy doors that opened outward. There was a small curb in the center of the driveway, and a red button on a curved piece of pipe. They inspected it, then looked around.

"Do you think we should press it?" asked Spiff.

"The map says the outlet's here," said Dud.

"I don't *see* anything…" said Jubee.

Suddenly there came a muffled horn and the door to the left swung open. The boys pressed themselves against the other door as two trucks labeled "Flint Catering Service" roared out and continued down the driveway. Their drivers waved to the Prohibition agents as they emerged onto the street. The kids, seeing the door about to close, quickly scurried through.

They were confronted with a further incline, another button, and some wooden steps that led up into a loft. Breaking some cobwebs, the boys mounted the steps and crossed the heavily-planked floor. On the side were some ancient barrels with faded letters: "Grand Traverse of Flint River, 1819." Hearing sounds, the boys crouched down, then lay prone and pulled themselves over to the edge.

They found themselves looking down into the inside of a small hill. Lights hung from the ceiling, illuminating a partial wall of massive wooden stakes and two or three log buildings of extreme age. In the center was an ancient cistern from which men were pulling an endless chain of barrels roped together. Those labeled "beer" were immediately shunted to a line of waiting trucks, while others labeled "brandy," "whisky," "gin," etc., were drained into an assembly line of moving bottles. They too were being boxed and loaded. Fully two dozen men were noisily at work, and several more stood guard.

Jubee spoke in awe. "It's an old trading post, maybe Jacob Smith's."

"Or a hidden fort left over from the French and Indian Wars," said Spiff.

"Being used by gangsters, right under everybody's nose," summed up Dud.

Spiff was incredulous. "This is where the liquor's coming from. This is how Slugsy makes his money." "And *that's* how it gets into the house," said Dud. He pointed to a platform holding different kegs, with pipes going down into the walls.

A factory whistle blew. "We'd better get out of here," said Jubee. The boys retreated, but nearing the bottom of the stairs they saw four guards leaving a small room on the other side of the garage doors. Two stood duty, while the others ambled towards them.

Dud signaled for his friends to follow, and they crossed over to an open doorway. They went down four steps into an empty room. To the right, more steps led down into a lower room, and two gangsters were climbing up. The boys were trapped.

The outside men entered and exchanged a few words with the men who were leaving, then descended into the lower area. The upper room was empty. The kids had disappeared.

Dud, Jubee and Spiff rapidly tripped downstairs from the trap door they had found only moments before. Below was a storage room with subdued light coming from an open door. Outside was a long hallway filled with boxes. They entered it, and a few steps down Dud thrust them through an opening. They were in their old room. The Time Machine was in the background. Dud quickly locked the door.

FORTS AND FANTASIES

"We're in our *own* room," said Spiff, amazed. "How…?"

"I *memorized* the map before we left," said Dud.

"We're safe here," said Jubee, relieved. "Nothing can happen to this room."

"Yes," said Spiff, "but something can happen to *us* if we're not careful. Let's leave Slugsy and his gang alone. Once Prohibition's over, they'll be history."

Jubee agreed. "Yes. We don't have much time left in 1929. And there's something else I want to do. Something I haven't told you about."

"What's that," his friends asked, closing around.

"I've already saved the Wizzer Automobile Company, so when we get back to 1991, my family should be rich. But there's something *else* I want to do.

"I want to *stop* the coming stock market crash. Stop it so there'll never be a Great Depression. Stop it so millions won't be out of work, so there won't be breadlines and kids going hungry every night."

"That's a tall order," said Dud, wondering if he could pass some gas.

"Do you think you can stop the crash?" said Spiff.

Jubee oozed confidence. "Before we left, I worked it all out on my Apple computer. It's all in this book, and the book's safe here. It's merely a matter of selective buying."

Dud was relieved and less enthusiastic. "We studied that in Mr. Hulett's class. All those rich dudes like J.P. Morgan tried to stop the crash. They had a thousand times the money you have, and they couldn't do it."

"That's true," said Jubee, glaring at Dud and opening the window. "The stock market will *have* to go down, to blow off all the *speculation*. But I have *hindsight*. I *know* what will happen. So I can use my money to make it an *orderly* retreat.

"For instance, I know that at a certain crucial time fifty thousand shares of U.S. Steel were thrown on the market for any price they'd bring. There were no buyers. Panic ensued, and the market plunged. If *I* buy them, stocks should rally.

"It's just a matter of the *right* buying at the *right* time. It's all psychological. That's what really runs Wall Street. *Psychology*, not money. It's all what people *think* will happen."

THE WONDERFUL EDISON TIME MACHINE

"Wow!" said Spiff.

"There's *one* certain day, and *one* certain hour, when everyone else was selling, that if someone had purchased just *eighteen* crucial stocks, the market would have turned. That's all it would have taken. Just *one* person, someone who had a vision and faith in his country's future, and the panic would have ended.

"I plan to be that person. I plan to be there on that day and at that time, right in the middle of the God-damned storm, and SAVE THIS FUCKING CENTURY!"

*   *   *   *   *

Evening found them in the Millionaires Club, enjoying milkshakes. Spiff was worried.

"You're going to be changing an awful lot of history if you prevent the stock market crash and the Great Depression. What'll happen in their *place*?"

Jubee licked his straw. "Probably better things. Maybe Hitler won't come to power, and there won't be a Second World War."

"Yes, but remember what Mr. Hulett said," Spiff continued, "about some good coming out of everything, even war. I know that blacks made real progress during World War II. A lot of them left the south to work in factories and shipyards. That's when *my* family came to Michigan.

"And the United Nations came into existence, and a lot of dictatorships fell. Even *Israel* was born."

"Fifty million people died in

[142]

FORTS AND FANTASIES

World War Two. And there was the Holocaust," said Jubee. "That's a heavy price to pay for progress. Maybe Israel could come about some other way. Maybe it could just be in every nation's heart."

"And maybe the Pope will turn Baptist," said Spiff. He turned to Dud, who was dreamily thumbing through Slugsy's ledger.

"What do you think, Dud? Is it smart for Jubee to be changing history?"

Dud was jolted back to reality. "No matter how much you change things," he said grimly, "*my folks* will still be poor. They've got poverty in their blood. Somebody should have kicked their asses fifty years ago. And," he said, mostly to himself, "I may be just the one to do it."

Jubee continued on. "I know it's taking a risk. But just imagine: no Depression, no war, and Hitler will remain a paperhanger…" His voice faded. Dud had returned to his reverie. A succession of "Albatross" headlines floated at him from an abyss.

DUD VERONA, KING OF RACKETS

FLINT CRIME CZAR CENTRAL HIGH TOUGH

GENESEE BLOODBATH: MOBSTERS ON RAMPAGE, with a photo of a careening touring car with machine guns sticking out. And finally:

BOOTLEG KING MASSACRES GANGSTER OPPONENTS, with a large photo of Dud.

His imagination moved in on the hidden gangster cave. Men were still at work, but all had jackets labeled "Dud Verona: Crime, Inc." with a yellow circle and a machine gun. The barrels emerging from the cistern said the same.

The ancient loft, now shored up with support columns, contained two gleaming copper vats for fermenting beer. A precision-like line of men was wheeling about wooden kegs labeled "Dud's Suds." Each contained a picture of a hand holding a foaming glass of beer. Dud, dressed as a gangster, stepped to the edge of the loft and looked down on his domain with harsh and glittering eyes.

Back in the Millionaires Club, the real Dud sighed, and the image went away.

CHAPTER TWENTY-FIVE

THE AQUINAS SOCIETY

The next day Dud stood in front of the same working-class house on East Street he would be born in forty-five years later. He was holding a sack.

The neighborhood hadn't changed much, but somehow it looked better. The same wan sunshine shone on faded paint and weathered window sills, but it seemed more mellow, even kind. There were no RV's squeezed in driveways, or canvas-covered boats. There were no blaring TV sets or heavy-mesh security doors. Children were actually playing in the street, and there was no profanity in their voices, only happiness. What cars were parked were mostly open ones, held together with hope and baling wire. But they had no Clubs on their steering wheels, or sophisticated alarm systems, and what contents they contained lay undisturbed.

Dud had a feeling he couldn't describe as he stood upon the porch and looked inside. The living room was much the same as in his time, the furnishings just closer to the original Sears catalogues. He recognized a lamp he'd broken twice himself, then was damaged once again when his father threw it at his mother. Above it was the Maxfield Parrish print family legend held was brought over on the Mayflower. It showed a land of timeless afternoon that a youthful Dud had always wanted to escape to. The bookcase held the same disheveled books purchased at long ago Chautauquas, or from encyclopedia salesmen whose straw hats and sunny dispositions spoke vaguely of things sensual, but who stayed in cheap hotel rooms, and took the next train out.

THE AQUINAS SOCIETY

A waspish woman was running a carpet sweeper. She looked up at Dud, who appeared a bit confused.

"I'm...I'm a distant relative," he stammered.

"You shoulda stayed distant," she said. "The icebox is straight ahead."

"I came to see...Mr. Verona."

"He's in the bathtub."

Dud took the stairs two at a time.

He went down a familiar hallway to a partly open door through which singing could be heard. The boy pushed it open, revealing his ancestor, happily stomping barefoot in the bathtub making gin. Stacked nearby were crates of rotten apples, over-ripe bananas, watermelon rinds, potato peelings, and bags of oats and barley. Several large funnels, crates of Mason jars and bottles of juniper juice were also close at hand.

"If you're here for a new batch," his relative said, "you're too early. It's got to age awhile. Come back in an hour."

Dud was nonplused. "You're making bathtub gin?"

"I hope to hell I am. If you've anything to contribute, don't use the toilet." Dud blanched. "Hand me those potato peelings." He sprinkled them in.

"I've heard you stomp grapes to make wine," said Dud, weakly. "But bathtub gin...?"

"Not everybody takes the time. That's why I'm able to *bond* my stuff. 'Feet' are the secret ingredient." He held up one foot. "That and washing your socks in it."

Dud showed his exasperation. "Look, Mr. Verona. I'm a relative of yours. This is small time. Prohibition isn't going to last forever, and then where will you be? Your feet will have rotted by that time. Plan ahead. Make yourself some *real dough*, so when liquor's legal, you'll be ready. You can own a chain of breweries, and your family will be *rich*."

Verona had Dud help him out of the tub, then threw in a few watermelon rinds and began stirring the mess with a broom. "So how am I going to do that?" he asked.

"By taking over the rackets in this town."

Verona laughed. "Slugsy controls the rackets in *this* town."

"Not anymore he don't," said Dud. "I've got the goods on *him*." He extended Slugsy's ledger. "In here's the name of every mobster in his gang. Every politician in his pay, and every speakeasy account in town. Plus how and where he gets his booze. Believe me, we can take him."

"*We?*"

"You and me and the hundred thousand dollars in this sack to get us started."

Verona peered into the sack. "You got my attention," he said. "And you look dumb enough to be a Verona. But a thing like this takes *thought*. I'll have to talk it over with my buddies at the Aquinas Society."

THE AQUINAS SOCIETY

"*The Aquinas Society*?"

"It's a men's group. We meet every Tuesday night for Bible study. It's the only thing my wife will let me out for."

"We don't need some wimp *religious* organization," protested Dud. "We need *real men*."

Verona gently relieved Dud of the sack of money. "It starts at eight o'clock. Why not stay for dinner, son. We're having ravioli."

*　　*　　*　　*　　*

Not long thereafter, Dud and his relation were walking down a deserted skid row street. They stopped by a door above which was a lighted cross and the words "Aquinas Society: Sympathy For the Poor."

"Too bad I forgot my prayer book," muttered Dud.

They went through a deserted foyer with a few saccharine religious pictures and opened a door. The room was filled with smoke, billiard tables, and the roughest characters east of Chicago. They all glared expectantly at the two figures in the doorway.

Verona emptied the sack of money and the ledger onto a table.

"There *is* a God!" said Dud.

CHAPTER TWENTY-SIX

GANGLAND DAYS

Midnight — several weeks later. A string of Lincoln touring cars edged their way down a deserted country road, their headlights masked to narrow slits of light. Their drivers, wary and determined, were illuminated dimly by the dashboard instruments, as were the guards, whose words had long since given way to tension and who gazed in silence out into the night.

Their cargo was booze, which people of all classes craved. Booze, the lubricant of social life, corrupter of officials, succor to the weak and helpless, giver of false gaiety and friends. Booze, which made the bad seem bearable, which brought forgetfulness and unfilled promises of better days to come. Booze, the devil in a drinking glass, wrecker of home and health, destroyer of loved ones, the elixir of death in rainbow colors. Booze, since time began, the gift of a cruel, benevolent God.

Booze, shipped down the lochs from Europe's great distilleries, packed in the holds of ocean-going ships, transferred in the New World to a flotilla of small boats that, swift in fog and night, braved their way to unmapped bays and bayous.

Booze, wending its way overland in a trail of violence and bloodshed to its final destination in a country wracked in the throes of Prohibition, noblest of experiments, which pitted man against his nature in a vain and winless war.

And now they drove, these men, unsurely, in the final place where no longer could a hand be bribed, and there were only predators. Dawn was a distant promise, and men would die this night, alone, unknown, in muck, outside the rule of law, with no blind Homer to extol them.

Ahead, Dud and his cohorts waited. Sounds of the approaching convoy reached him, and he gave a sign. Headlamps from five cars that blocked the highway sprang to life, blinding those approaching. Gunfire wracked them and they spun out of control into a ditch. Like a modern Robin Hood, Dud then led his men in the attack.

* * * * *

There was a warehouse filled with booze. Its guard looked at a skylight. A hooded, caped figure was crouching there. The guard activated a siren and from below, gangsters in a poker game poured out a door. Dud swept down and cut a rope holding a suspended flat of empty beer kegs. The kegs demolished the gangsters as Dud's men burst in with cans of gasoline. As the warehouse was consumed in flames, they escaped into the night.

Several evenings later — Flint's most elegant gambling establishment, the one with carpeting on the floor. A beautiful woman had just put chips down on a roulette table. Dud suavely moved in and placed an even greater pile on her bet. The wheel was spun, and the lady won. She kissed him seductively, then gave him the key to her room. She departed with a promising smile as Dud casually dropped it in a box that held a dozen others. He then nodded his head, and members of his gang crashed through the doors and began to smash the equipment.

A bookie joint — racing charts, people on phones, a haze of smoke, and a wire cage where money was being counted. Pops, an arthritic old man, had just taken a large bag of cash to a nearby room where big shots were having drinks beside a window.

He dumped the bills on a desk, then as the men began to count it, deftly unsnapped a window latch. Outside, men edged their way across a parapet. They leaped into the room as "Pops" ripped off his mask, revealing himself as *Dud*. The big shots raised their hands.

THE WONDERFUL EDISON TIME MACHINE

*   *   *   *   *

The following evening, Dud and Jubee were relaxing in the lounge of the Millionaires Club. Jubee was reading the latest headline of the "Flint Albatross."

DUD'S THUGS MUG LOCAL LUGS — MOB WAR BLOODIES CITY STREETS.

"Doesn't it bother you to be breaking the law?" he inquired of his friend.

"No more than it does you to be manipulating the stock market."

"I'm trying to create a better world," Jubee said.

"Well, if they want any booze in this 'better world,'" Dud replied, "they'll have to come to me."

*   *   *   *   *

Hours later, on a downtown Flint street, women of doubtful reputation were being led into a paddy wagon from a padlocked nightclub. Two reporters were watching.

"That's the *sixth place* Verona's closed this week," said one of them. "Slugsy sure ain't gonna like it. He used to have this town sewn up."

The other one shivered. "Yeah! I understand Dud's sending him an ultimatum: *Surrender Your Rackets Or Die*."

The first one turned to go. "I'm gonna find me a nice little war in Asia to cover. I don't want to be around when Slugsy gets *that!*"

*   *   *   *   *

Slugsy, the object of their fear and loathing, lived on the top floor of the Gas House Social Club in Brick Town, a disreputable section of Detroit, which in itself vied with Chicago and New York as the nation's citadel of sin. The building was shabby and run down, but his digs were palatial, and from them he controlled a crime syndicate that permeated the entire state of Michigan.

From Grosse Ile to Grosse Pointe, mayors, aldermen, vestrymen, commissioners, turnkeys, tosspots, justices, tenured professors, surrogates, sacristans, even sommeliers and subalterns — all were subservient to him,

SLUGSY LIVED ON THE TOP FLOOR OF THE GAS HOUSE SOCIAL CLUB IN DETROIT.

held in an iron grip of terror and remuneration. Fish grew plump on those who didn't comply, and the fields of daisies that ringed the city bore fragrant witness to his vengeance.

This morning the resident crime lord was scanning the latest headlines while having breakfast with his moll. Both were eating grapefruit.

"Na-a-a-a-a-a," the gangster growled. "Take over *my* rackets, will he? Well, it's venetian blinds for *him*."

"Curtains, Slugsy, you mean *curtains*," his moll corrected.

"It says Verona's sending me a…a 'ulta-matum!'" Oh he is, the wise guy. Well, I'll send him one *right back*." He turned to the woman. "Find me an ultamatum, *my* size," he instructed.

"I can't even find a *jock strap* your size," she replied.

Slugsy made to bean her with his grapefruit, but this time she was prepared, and quickly donned a catcher's mask. So he grabbed a nearby seltzer bottle and squirted her instead.

CHAPTER TWENTY-SEVEN

AN INTERIM

Back in Flint, Spiff, dressed in work clothes and carrying a bag, approached the George Willoughby mansion. The Prohibition agent turned from waving catering trucks carrying liquor off the premises and glared at him.

"What you got in that bag, black boy?" he demanded. He pulled out a bottle and smelled it. "ALCOHOL!"

"That's *rubbing* alcohol," said Spiff. "Mr. Meadowcroft has a sore back."

The agent tossed the bottle back to Spiff, then gave him a swift kick, sending boy and bag into the dirt.

"See if it's good for sore butts, too," he laughed, and turned away.

A few moments later Spiff was in a dingy lavatory, washing off. Jubee entered through the door.

"I *thought* I heard a noise."

"How's it going?" Spiff asked.

"Okay! We don't see much of you these days."

"I don't want to be a gangster," the boy said, sadly. "And I don't know shit about the stock market."

Jubee wiped some dirt off him. "So what ya been doing?"

"I've been helping David and the others rebuild the Playboy."

"You don't know anything about cars, either," Jubee observed.

"I took auto shop at Central."

"Yes, but all you made was an all-purpose hubcap remover," his friend replied. Spiff brightened a bit. "Well, it sure came in handy at Open House, remember?"

"I'll say," Jubee agreed. "Half the teachers at Central are still driving around with the wrong hubcaps, but they're too dumb to know it."

Both boys were laughing now as they exited the lavatory and entered the secret room. It was filled with charted stocks and graphs.

"You're really serious about this stock market thing, aren't you?" Spiff said.

"You bet. Next Tuesday is September 3, 1929. That's the day the market will reach its highest point, 381. It will then go all the way down to 41, wiping out the investments of millions of people and helping cause the greatest depression in history. It'll be a *quarter century* before the market comes back."

"Can you stop all that?" asked Spiff.

"Remember, I *know* what's going to happen. With my help the worst of the speculation should be blown off without the market crashing. Then the 1930s can be a period of growth."

"Why don't you move all this to the Millionaires Club? You'd be more comfortable there."

"This is the only place that's safe. Since the Time Machine can't be destroyed, neither can anything else in this room." He flipped through a pile of slips. "I'm due to meet the bankers in a few hours. Next week I start to rewrite history."

* * * * *

The following week, a succession of "Albatross" headlines told the story. Readers could almost hear the din of Wall Street in the background.

STOCKS REACH NEW HIGHS

BABSON WARNS OF IMPENDING CRASH

DOWN DAY ON WALL STREET

SURPRISE BUYING ON FLINT EXCHANGE BUOYS MARKET

MYSTERIOUS MICHIGAN SYNDICATE SUPPORTING MARKET — WHERE IS MONEY COMING FROM?

THE WONDERFUL EDISON TIME MACHINE

Jubee worked late every night in the Time Machine room, surrounded by paperwork. One evening there was a small knock at the door. Spiff entered with a tray of milk and sandwiches.

"I saw the car outside. You'd better eat," he said.

Jubee took a bite of the sandwich. "How's the Playboy coming?"

"Slow but sure. You should see the quality. They don't build things that well in our time."

"I'd like to," Jubee said wearily. "But tomorrow's another one of those 'crucial days.' Prices are sliding, but there's no panic yet. I'm meeting the bankers at midnight. We've got to be ready by the opening bell. Things are heating up."

*   *   *   *   *

The Flint Stock Exchange was little like its sister edifice in New York, which cast its stately Greco-Roman portico so imposingly in the canyons of lower Manhattan. It was a modernistic building with an ordinary-size room containing 24 desks and an aisle down the middle. At the end was a raised platform with a master desk and a wall-to-wall board where young men frantically posted the latest price quotations derived from a bank of glass-topped tickers.

Outside, a small crowd had gathered. A limousine drove up and the three bankers emerged. Several reporters cornered them.

"Who do you represent? Are you still supporting the market? Any comments on the collapse of the Belgium Exchange?"

The bankers shook them off and entered the floor. All activity ceased and a multitude of faces looked at them — hope and hunger in their despairing eyes. The bankers advanced down the aisle dispersing Jubee's "buys" and "sells" like chickenfeed. The brokers grabbed their phones, and the cacophony of their voices soon rose to a crescendo.

CHAPTER TWENTY-EIGHT

SOMEWHERE WEST OF LARAMIE

There was a garden in Flint that few had ever seen. It lay behind protective walls and was a place of verdant lawns and flower beds, and trees that aged with grace and knew no fear.

Its paths were trails the woodland creatures made, and led through scented foliage to ponds whose shady depths held flashing gold. Milk-white statues rose above entwining ivy and got away with things that only statues can, and benches from lost palaces waited in the shadows of long afternoons for the rustle of forbidden love.

Drowsy delights were everywhere, and nature so in harmony that if a person cleared his soul and lay upon the breast of earth with half-closed eyes and mind made numb by dappled sunlight dancing through the leaves, he could hear, beneath it all, faint as a gossamer web and spinning without thought or time, the quiet industries of God.

It was only natural this garden belonged to Flint's crime lord, a heavyset older man who spoke like his mouth was full of mush. Today he was being approached by two of his local mobsters.

"You've been Slugsy's man in Flint for twenty years. You've got to take some action," the first one said.

"People are beginning to say you've sold out to Verona," said the second one.

The Don was barely intelligible, and spoke not much above a whisper.

"Calm down. I know what I'm doing." A little boy ran up pulling a small fabric-covered wagon. "Take a powder. I want to play with my grandson."

The two men kissed his ring and exited. The child's hand pulled back the covering, revealing stacks of hundred dollar bills. The Don reached for the money. Lucian turned and beamed proudly, then held out a long, unfolded steamship ticket.

*   *   *   *   *

An ocean voyage later, two men stood in front of an armchair in a luxurious library. They were both well-dressed and well-bred, and they looked expectantly at a man in the armchair, who cleared his throat and then spoke in impeccable English:

"The lint — in Flint — gives hint — of peppermint."

"By George," enthused the men, "I think he's got it."

The Don held out his hand as through the window came the sound of Big Ben tolling the hour.

*   *   *   *   *

Back in Flint, things weren't going quite as well. Big Louie blew his whistle in alarm. He was overseer of the cistern area in the hidden cave, and Dud's men were rushing in. After lukewarm fisticuffs, Slugsy's workers raised their hands, demoralized.

*   *   *   *   *

Elsewhere, cartons of Dud's Suds were being lugged into a bar, while a man smashed a beer keg with an axe. A gangster presented a reluctant bartender with an invoice.

*   *   *   *   *

The Millionaires Club had stringent laws against all things temporal invading its domain, so its dining room was hushed, above the fray engulfing Flint. Jubee and Spiff were having breakfast, their pinkies held in just the right position. The former looked up and saw Lucian passing an archway, carrying a guillotine.

SOMEWHERE WEST OF LARAMIE

"Why is Lucifer here?" he asked.

Spiff, buttering his toast in tiny squares, looked across the room. Lucian was now carrying a large cat in the same direction.

"He's been suspended from school for two days," was his reply.

"Whatever for?" inquired Jubee.

"For turning his homework in on time."

There was a screech from the archway, and the cat went running back. The three bankers were crossing the room. They nodded to Spiff and pulled up chairs. Cardington was the first to speak.

"Your madness is causing us problems. For weeks now we haven't been able to phone in your stock orders because our lines are being tapped by jealous brokers."

"We tried private messengers," Worthington added. "But within three days they accept large bribes and retire to Bermuda."

"And when *we* go, we're mobbed by the press," said Greenwich. "It's bad publicity for the bank to have its officials seen publicly speculating in the stock market."

"You'll *have* to find another way to get your orders in," concluded Cardington. "And it'll have to be good. Half the city is trying to get an inside tip on what you're going to do."

Jubee looked over at the archway. "I'll see what I can do."

* * * * *

The next morning, reporters were milling about outside the stock exchange, waiting for the bankers to show up. Lucian, dressed as a ragamuffin shoeshine boy, came walking down the sidewalk playing with his yo-yo and carrying a wooden kit. Unnoticed, he entered the exchange and moved down the aisle, handing out envelopes. At the end, he put his yo-yo down and handed a cluster more to the man at the tall desk. Hours later came the headlines:

TURMOIL ON STOCK EXCHANGE

The Wonderful Edison Time Machine

SHOESHINE BOY PUTS LIFE SAVINGS OF $200,000,000 IN MARKET
WALL STREET BREATHLESS — CAN PRICES HOLD?

* * * * *

The relief of evening finally came. Jubee and Margaret were walking along the beach. They passed Mr. Gatsby, who was using a navy signal shutter to flash a message across the lake.

"You seem awfully worried," Margaret said.

"I am," her boyfriend replied. "In the next three weeks I'm going to put more money in the stock market than the Federal government's *entire* budget."

"Daddy says Hoover's spending too much money as it is." Margaret stopped. "Don't forget. John McCormack's singing at our house tonight."

"Oh, yeah," said Jubee, as they continued on. "I couldn't forget an important thing like that."

* * * * *

David and Spiff, exhausted, were in the greenhouse sharing a soft drink. The unfinished Wizzer Playboy gleamed in the background. Derby was asleep on a pile of excelsior. David was in a reflective mood.

"The Playboy is more than an automobile, Spiff. It's a way of life. It's four wheels of freedom on a never-ending highway in the first light of dawn.

"I'll tell you something I've never told anyone before. When I was your age, or maybe even younger, I was at a ranch out in Wyoming. One evening, right about sunset, I saw a girl coming back from the corral. She'd just broken a horse, and her face was smudged and her clothes were dirty, but her hair was ablaze from the setting sun. And she walked — How can I say it? Like she owned the world.

"I never saw her again. But somewhere west of Laramie there's a bronco-busting, steer-roping girl who knows what I'm talking about. She knows what a sassy pony can do when it's a cross between greased lightning and two thousand pounds of steel and action, and it's tearing down the wind high, wide and handsome.

Somewhere West of Laramie

"The truth is — the Playboy was built for her."

"That's beautiful," said Spiff.

*   *   *   *   *

Dud was with his fellow gangsters in a touring car.

"So it's finally ready, eh?" he said.

"Yeah! The Don moved out in a hurry. But we had to renovate it, you know — make it good enough for you."

"Well, get this crate moving," Dud demanded. "I can hardly wait to see it."

*   *   *   *   *

The Never-Ending Party was going strong, much like a frenzied train hell-bent for oblivion. There was more recklessness and more abandon, and people somehow sensed it was the end of things. Worried knots of men discussed the stock market, while their wives clutched costly jewels and bemoaned the rise in crime. There was a larger crowd than usual around the magic fountain, and the stairs were thick with supplicants who searched with sad and hollow eyes for things which never would return.

As always, the great Corinthian columns and majestic ceilings looked down like sentinels upon the doomed, who ebbed and flowed like waves from a retreating sea, and waited for the sound of tumbrels in the night.

John McCormack, the world-famous Irish tenor, had been imported at great expense to sing this evening, and there was scattered applause when he stepped out onto a platform. He sang "Queen of the May," and his rich voice spoke of emerald bays in an impoverished land where women waited on high bluffs for their lads across the sea. It spoke of unpicked roses blown in autumn gales, and whitewashed farms on windy hills whose frugal smoke was quickly lost in emptiness.

It had the sound of brooks that tumbled past old monuments, whose moss-filled runes were meaningless except to those who slept beneath the sod. It spoke of peasants rich in poverty, tilling fields as barren as God's promises, of weary plowmen wending their way home at dusk of evensong. It sang the warmth of a simple meal, the welcome of a friendly hearth, the sound of porter being shared, and gnarled hands with rosaries.

Jubee and Margaret too felt things had gone wrong, but they held hands and bravely smiled as the party flashed and swirled around them. Dud was preening himself in his new gangster headquarters, a magnificent high-windowed office with a Louis XVI desk. David and Spiff were asleep at their workbenches. With the ending of the song the mansion, with all its lights, receded until clouds rolled in and only the moon shone down.

CHAPTER TWENTY-NINE

FROM PROMETHEAN HEIGHTS

The next morning Slugsy was again eating grapefruit in Detroit and scowling at the latest "Albatross" headline: "Secret Gangland Meeting Today — Slugsy To Unite Warring Factions." He tossed the paper over to his moll, who was wearing a welder's mask.

"Secret gangland meeting, huh?" he sneered. "Nobody invited *me* to this big confab. But Slugsy'll be there. Yeah! He'll be there *in spades.*"

He snapped his fingers and a butler brought his revolver on a silver tray. He strapped it on, then turned and struck his moll.

"*In spades*, you cast-iron cu- OW, OW, OW, W, W, W, W, W, W, W!"

He left the room in agony.

*   *   *   *   *

Hours later, streams of gangsters were being admitted into the hidden cave. Dud was addressing a squad of guards just inside the heavy garage doors and showing them a drawing of the notorious Slugsy.

"Remember: If it looks like this, don't let it in. Search every incoming car. Look under every hood. Check every hood. Don't let anything like this in."

Just up the incline, in the cistern area, workers were taking newly-emerged barrels to a nearby stack. Moments later the end of one cautiously pivoted, and Slugsy himself looked out.

The meeting area was a conventional room a few steps down from the cistern. A fair-sized chandelier hung from the ceiling, and a hundred or so gangsters were milling about, divided into hostile factions that eyed each other suspiciously. There was an elevated head table where Dud's relative and several Aquinas members sat, plus Dud's "secretary" (now his moll), and Lucian, dressed as Slugsy, idly going through a stack of papers. Dud entered and sat down.

"Listen, shrimp ball. We start in ten minutes. You're not to say a word. Just glare at everyone and nod up and down at everything I say. Make like you're working on these papers of Slugsy's. *And don't light your cigar!*"

Lucian whispered something in Dud's ear. The older boy frowned and pointed. The little boy happily skipped away.

Moments later, Lucian was emerging from the restroom. He passed an open archway just as Slugsy did. Lucian began to jump up and down, but Slugsy yanked him through the opening.

"We've done that shtick before," he said.

He strong-armed the boy through a storage room and tossed him into a closet. He then locked the door and threw away the key. Inside there was momentary darkness, and then light. Lucian had pulled out his new yo-yo, which lit up. He took from his back pocket a copy of "Locks and Safes of the Western World" by Dr. John Hooey, selected a wire from a number contained within its spine, and set to work.

Slugsy swaggered down the hall and entered the meeting area. Dud waved him over frantically. "Did you have it in crossways?" he demanded, and shoved the gangster down into a seat. Slugsy glowered evilly, moved a machine gun close to him, and lit a cigar. Dud made to stop him, but one of his henchmen rang a glass and rose to speak.

"All right, youse guys. Settle down. We're here for a meetin', an *important* meetin'. One that's going to make *peace* for *everybody* in the rackets. There's gonna be plenty for all, and Slugsy ain't gonna cause no more trouble. In fact, he's *all for* this."

From Promethean Heights

There was opposition in the audience.

"How do we know you ain't full of it?" cried one gangster. "We take our orders from Slugsy. And he ain't told us nothin' 'bout no Versailles peace meetin'." He turned to derisive laughter from his cohorts.

Dud's speaker reassured them. "Slugsy himself is gonna give you the okay right *here, today*. The okay to join in with Dud Verona and *really* make crime pay." The room broke out in cheers.

Outside, Lucian exited the closet and headed directly for a telephone. He stood on a box and made a call.

Back in the meeting room, Dud's relative was summing up.

"So that's it. A clean sweep. Slugsy keeps Detroit; our mob takes all the rest, except for Ann Arbor, where we can't compete with the sororities. There's vice enough for everyone, and all you mugs can join."

Some of the hoods were unconvinced. One of them aimed a gun at the head table. "Let's check this first with Slugsy. You say he's here. *Let's see him*."

Dud rose and smiled nervously. "A fair request. And without further ado, heeeeeeeere's *SLUGSY*." He swooped his hand exuberantly, then went to lift a paper. "He's a little hoarse today, so he's asked me to read his speech."

Slugsy climbed onto the table, machine gun now in hand, mean as roofing nails. "Boys…" he began, but the mobsters were beside themselves with laughter.

"*That* shrimp? He ain't four feet tall!" "That's not Slugsy. He's still in diapers."

Slugsy crouched and fired his gun at the chandelier. The gangsters dove as crystal splattered everywhere. The destroyed chandelier rose, as another one descended. The audience unsteadily regained its feet.

"We didn't mean nothin'." "If you say you're Slugsy…"

Lucian leaped onto the platform and grabbed Slugsy's machine gun. He sprayed the new chandelier, and the gangsters were again showered. He took the cigar from Slugsy's mouth and stood triumphantly as a new chandelier dropped down. Dud shook his head in despair.

THE WONDERFUL EDISON TIME MACHINE

The mobsters regained their feet and, now holding umbrellas, were in consternation.

"*TWO* Slugsies? Which one is the *right* one?"

One hood spoke high above the others. "I hear the *real* Slugsy has a 'Mom' tattoo he's proud of."

Slugsy rolled up his sleeve and showed his "Mom" tattoo, flexing his muscles at the same time. All eyes then turned to Lucian. The boy indicated "It's a cinch." He turned his back and dropped his pants. His "Mom" tattoo was bared to acclamation.

Stymied, another gangster had his say. "I heard the *real* Slugsy is a yo-yo expert."

Slugsy removed his yo-yo and did a number of involved tricks. He ended to spirited applause. Lucian then pulled out *his* yo-yo and indicated the room should darken with his finger. It simultaneously did, and he performed even more complicated tricks, and *his* yo-yo *lit* up. "Oohs" and "aahs" came from the felons.

Dud was not pleased. "They don't *have* lighted yo-yos in 1929," he hissed to Lucian.

"They do now," the lad replied.

His performance ended to even louder applause as the lights returned. But indecisiveness still reigned.

"This ain't gettin' us nowhere," yelled another hood. "How about something only Slugsy would know — namely, *who killed Louie the Lug*?"

"*Well, boys,*" said Slugsy confidently, pushing Lucian aside, "I can take credit for that. Louie crossed me, see? And *nobody* crosses Slugsy, see? He was trying to muscle in, take over. So I called him in. Nice friendly chat. Told him what he could expect if he stayed loyal. Well, he said he wanted more than promises. He wanted something *concrete*. So I gave him something *concrete*. Now he's feeding fishes at the bottom of the Detroit River, the same as you mugs if you don't *get smart!*"

From Promethean Heights

There were more cheers. Slugsy turned to Lucian. The boy gulped and rifled through the papers on the table. Selecting one, he triumphantly unrolled…Louie the Lug's *Death Certificate*. Louder cheers resulted.

A future candidate for MENSA waved them quiet. "I know what to do. The *real* Slugsy would like to kill this Dud Verona. So let's give *both* a chance and see what happens."

Dud's men were covered as a machine gun was handed to Lucian. Dud was placed against a wall, where he sweated and fidgeted as he attempted to protect his vital parts, most of which were apparently below the waist.

As all the gangsters strained to see, Lucian aimed the gun at Dud. But he could not bring himself to fire, and he lowered it. The weapon was then handed to Slugsy, who caressed it obscenely and turned to fire at the trembling boy.

Outside on the street, Spiff was carrying a package. He noted a yellow Montahooey school bus pulling up. Out of it poured forty kids dressed as Slugsy. Spiff could not believe his eyes. Led by a swashbuckling Dr. Hooey, the students charged up the driveway with tumultuous cries. A catering truck had just left the hideout, and it swerved to avoid hitting some of the youthful invaders. There was a crashing sound as a case of liquor fell to the ground.

The two younger Prohibition agents took immediate note of this. They looked at the truck, then up the driveway. Suddenly things dawned on them. They grabbed their axes and rushed up the incline. Dr. Hooey had already activated the mechanism, and the kids were all inside.

Slugsy was about to pull the trigger. It was his first kill of the day, and he wanted to enjoy it. Dud's brief life passed before him like a bad X-rated movie. The room was taut — then forty imitation Slugsies stormed inside. Dr. Hooey snatched the gun from the startled gangster. Kids were all over the place, and the mobsters were incredulous. They rolled up the sleeves of those they could catch, and pulled down the pants of others, each time revealing a "Mom" tattoo. No one could tell who the real Slugsy was, and no one knew what to do.

The Wonderful Edison Time Machine

Spiff wandered up the driveway and stepped inside the hideout. It was always an experience seeing what the white folks were doing. He saw that the two Prohibition agents were earnestly chopping down the wooden supports holding up the loft and its two large metal vats. Already dust and debris were sifting down.

The gangsters now had Dr. Hooey covered. All the Slugsies were lined up, and Dud again the target. The machine gun was tossed to the first kid, then the second, and then the third. All refused it. The real Slugsy recoiled in disgust.

The Prohibition agents had kicked away the supports they severed, and had begun on more. There was a wrenching, groaning noise as planks began to buckle, and Spiff was drenched in a waterfall of beer.

The real Slugsy was now third in line. The two before him quickly flunked the test, and he was again given the weapon. Dud sensed he faced the real McCoy and said a prayer to those few saints he knew as Slugsy raised the gun.

With a final push, the Prohibition agents demolished the last supports, and the vats began to fall. Dumbstruck, the two men fled toward the meeting area. Spiff raced down the slope to the outside driveway and managed to close the doors just as the entire loft came crashing down. He covered his ears and grimaced at the noise.

From Promethean Heights

Slugsy's finger was just pulling the trigger when the crash came. The Prohibition agents burst in, followed by a seething wall of beer. Pandemonium broke out, and everyone dashed panic-stricken for the doors on the other side of the room, which led to the beach.

In the cistern area the tossing, foaming maelstrom had already destroyed the special apparatus for conveying liquor to the magic fountain, and was swirling in a vortex down into the lower area where the kids once disappeared. From there it broke through walls and roared unchallenged down the hallway toward the secret room, sweeping all before it.

Inside the Never-Ending Party, guests assembled by the magic fountain were astonished when its life-giving waters dwindled and then ceased.

In the meeting area people were pulling each other through the beer and floating chairs and pouring out to the safety of the beach in one big mangled mess.

Spiff was further down the driveway, standing by the broken case of liquor. Suddenly he was cuffed and sent sprawling. It was the head Prohibition agent.

"Okay, black boy! You reek of beer. Tell me where's the rest of it, or I'll beat the daylights out of you."

Spiff looked up at him and shrugged.

"Right — through — that — door!"

The agent rushed up the drive, pressed the button, and waited expectantly.

Gunfire had broken out on the beach as Dud's men fled in all directions. Amid the confusion, the Central High Capone, his relative and Lucian all broke track records as they escaped down the sand. They collided with Gatsby, who was helping a demure fat lady in a wedding dress, a minister and four nasty children emerge from a rowboat. All went sprawling into the water, and when they surfaced, soggy and bedraggled, they too took after the three fleeing figures.

The Prohibition agent again pressed the button. Nothing happened. He angrily turned to Spiff, who was stretched out on top of the driveway wall. The boy obligingly called to him:

"Try kicking the door."

The agent did, and it opened, releasing a tidal wave of beer that swept the astonished agent in a cataract of suds down the driveway and out into the street. Spiff waved at him as he went by, then, when the flood subsided, regained his package and went whistling on his way.

AFTERMATH

Jubee, Dud and Spiff were walking amid the wreckage in the garage area. They came upon the Time Machine, smashed almost beyond recognition. Spiff looked at it sadly.

"You told us it couldn't be destroyed."

"But it is," said Dud.

Jubee picked up the soaked remnants of his stock statistics book. Most of its pages were missing. "I'm afraid we're marooned here," he said.

"Marooned?" said Dud.

"In 1929," said Jubee.

"It'll be thirty years before I can eat another Big Mac," wailed Spiff.

Dud joined in the lamentation. "*Playboy* won't start publishing centerfolds until I'm too old to care."

"I'm sorry," Jubee said. "I don't know what went wrong. Apparently we changed things just by being here."

"Edison's still alive," said Spiff. "There was an article on him in *Time*. Maybe he can build us a new one."

"Edison doesn't even know his Time Machine works. Because when he turned it on in 1910, nothing happened. It was too new; it had no past. You need an *old* machine, one that's been around for years. This one had *eighty years* of past in 1991. So we were able to use it. *Only it* was programmed to return us, and now it's wrecked."

From Promethean Heights

It began to rain.

"I knew if we stayed here long enough, it'd start to rain," Spiff said.

Dud was remorseful. "This is all my fault. Me and my big ideas."

"No, said Jubee. "It's my fault. I'm the one responsible. Now we're stuck here. And tomorrow is 'Black Thursday,' the first day of the stock market crash. Without my book I don't know what to do."

"You should have copied it at Kinko's," said Spiff.

"The don't have them yet," said Jubee.

He threw away the few pages that remained. The three boys looked forlornly at the debris and then moved on.

CHAPTER THIRTY

THE END OF A
WONDERFUL ERA

Newsboys in knickerbockers shouted the news on the transfixed streets of Flint, and people snatched the papers from their grubby hands, often not waiting for change.

WILD DAY ON WALL STREET

STOCKS PLUNGE IN FRENZIED TRADING

MARKET DESPERATE FOR SUPPORT

Under the porte cochere of the Millionaires Club the Rolls-Royce purred softly as Jubee placed his latest stock orders in Lucian's shoeshine kit. Spiff and Dud waited in attendance.

"All I can do is *guess* which stocks to buy," he said. "But several billion dollars *should* make a difference." He patted Lucian on the head and ushered him into the car.

Police were holding back the crowds of curious as Lucian's car drove up before the Stock Exchange. Inside, pandemonium reigned, but it ceased when the little boy entered. As he began distributing his new stock orders, cheers broke out. At the tall end table he put down his yo-yo and extended a fistful more.

Behind a nearby door two men pushed out a little girl. She was dressed as Mata Hari, and with uncertain grace she sauntered over to Lucian and gave him a smile. This was frosting on the young boy's cake, and he took her arm and escorted her back down the aisle.

THE END OF A WONDERFUL ERA

Outside, with instincts honed from a million years of femininity, she immediately spied an ice cream parlor with a sign announcing sodas. She indicated her desire by tugging on his arm and he willingly complied, even gallantly opening the door for her. Once inside, he appraised the menu carefully while a waiter deftly removed his kit.

In the back room the waiter joined the original two men, who paid him off. Then they hastily removed the contents of the kit: a copy of *Children's Activities* a baseball, an apple core, a Dr. Hooey tract on how to raise bail, and a decoder badge with sheets of numbers. The last two items were eagerly seized.

The two children finished their soda in a way unapproved by Emily Post,  and the waiter returned the kit and presented the bill. Lucian gravely considered it, then shoved it across the table to his new-found girlfriend and left.

In the following few days Jubee marshaled his remaining money as would a general his troops on a great battlefield. He made endless computations and bit his pencil to a stub, and each day Lucian delivered his Delphic decisions to a cheering stock exchange. But in the end, like the birds in Flint's now autumn skies, it all went south in margin calls.

THE WONDERFUL EDISON TIME MACHINE

* * * * *

Somewhere, in a smoke-filled room, four men were trying to make sense of Lucian's figures. They were knee-deep in adding machines, wadded paper and seltzer bottles.

FIRST MAN: "1254620…that could mean the 125th stock down, buy at 46, twenty thousand shares."

SECOND MAN: "Try it. Phone it in."

FIRST MAN: "Or it could mean sell."

SECOND MAN: "Then sell it. We have to crack this code."

THIRD MAN: (working with decoder) "I keep getting 'Ovaltine.'"

FOURTH MAN: "That's it. *OVALTINE!* It's the *letters*, see… "O" — Olympia Oil; "V" — Viceroy Tobacco; "A" — Amalgamated Airlines; "L"…there's several "L's."

FIRST MAN: "Buy them all."

SECOND MAN: "Sell them all."

THIRD MAN: "Maybe it's the *numbers* on the boxes."

FOURTH MAN: "What boxes?"

THIRD MAN: (holding one up) "*Ovaltine* boxes."

FOURTH MAN: "Order a truckload."

The third man grabbed a phone.

* * * * *

Now, each day, the hard work, sweat and toil of a hundred million people melted like the wings of Icarus in a gale of numbers and chicanery. Values vanished to a netherworld of smoke and mirrors, and it was as if a cabal of criminals had broken into Eden and stolen the gifts of God.

* * * * *

The four men were more frantic than ever. Workmen were wheeling cartons of Ovaltine in, against a wall of them.

FOURTH MAN: (checking boxes) "I'm beginning to see a pattern."

The FIRST MAN threw down his pencil. "It's too late. We're down three

THE END OF A WONDERFUL ERA
===

hundred million dollars. We'll have to sell tomorrow for whatever we can get."

The next day was Tuesday, October 29, 1929 — "Black Tuesday," scheduled to be the most destructive day in U.S. financial history.

A bewildered mob of hapless investors encamped in front of the New York Stock Exchange, and the street itself was closed. In buildings proudly soaring skyward, those in the know reserved their window ledges or wired Wenatchee for the latest quotes on apples. Papers rushed from still-wet presses which offered any kindling of hope were desperately devoured by men who saw their homes, their families, their lives, the economic system they had so long believed in, even the ground they stood upon, sinking beneath their eyes.

Hands shook as they read the headlines:

STOCKS HOLDING

EYES OF WORLD ON FLINT OPENING

SHOESHINE BOY HOLDS KEY TO NATION'S PROSPERITY (with a photo of Lucian and his kit).

* * * * *

The four boys were standing under the porte cochere of the Millionaires Club. Jubee had bad news for them.

"We're wiped out, broke, kaput! We haven't got a dime."

The Rolls drew up, and he gave the driver its title.

"I had to let Jenkins go. And I have to let the car go, too."

"You mean we ain't got wheels?" protested Dud.

"No, we 'ain't got wheels,'" said Jubee, mimicking him. "But we still have feet, and I have a feeling we'll be needing them."

The concierge approached and aloofly presented the boy with an overdue bar bill. Jubee glanced at it scornfully.

"*Two hundred dollars for eight hundred milkshakes?* Don't bother me with trifles." He waved the man aside. Meanwhile, Lucian had whispered something to the chauffeur. The man nodded "yes" and the little boy entered the car and it drove away. The older boys were too preoccupied to notice.

THE WONDERFUL EDISON TIME MACHINE

Newsreel cameramen, radio announcers, flash photographers, reporters: *all* had besieged the humble Flint Stock Exchange and were held back only by a thin brave line of State troopers. Lucian looked small in the back seat of the limousine, and he emerged hesitatingly, kit and all. He walked into the exchange and all activity stopped. It was like a waxworks, where horrible crimes are frozen in suspended animation. The desks were manned by gargoyles, whose naked faces revealed the basest fears and truths. The very air was charged, and time itself a victim.

The boy passed the first row of desks, and although the brokers' lips were dry and pleading, there was naught for them. He passed the second row, and its denizens knew there'd now be no reprieve. He passed the third, and it was as if a shadow followed him, blotting out all rational thought and sanity.

Lucian reached the tall desk at the end. There was no sound. He put his kit upon the table. The man leaned down. The little boy whispered in his ear. The man took an item from his desk and handed it to him. It was his yo-yo.

Lucian backed up, turned, and ran. Everyone looked at him and then each other. Then came the cries in waves:

"Sell; sell; sell at market. Sell at any price. *Sell; sell; sell.*"

Apocalyptic headlines told the story:

MARKET CRASHES

MILLIONS LOSE LIFE SAVINGS

END OF A WONDERFUL ERA

WALL STREET LAYS AN EGG.

When midnight came to the deserted floor of the stock exchange, a shaft of moonlight illuminated the waste of tickertape, sell orders and soiled paper cups, all of which would be swept up in the cold tomorrow. Amid the debris of a million broken dreams was Lucian's battered shoeshine kit.

LUCIAN WALKED INTO THE STOCK EXCHANGE AND ALL ACTIVITY STOPPED.

The End of a Wonderful Era

* * * * *

The time was even later, and the night as closed as a miser's purse, when at the rear of the Millionaires Club four silk hats were thrown down, and then a rope. Dud shinnied down, and a trunk was lowered to him. Then Jubee and Spiff descended, and all three boys lifted the trunk and disappeared into the gloom.

Some hours later the older boys were in the Bum's Rush flophouse, sitting on a bed. Its sheets were stained with unfamiliar odors, and they were lonely and afraid. The place was run by an older man with watery eyes who slobbered at them from a nearby doorway and said he had some doughnuts in his room. He was called "Bung Hole," not without reason, and the kids were warned to sleep in shifts. Lucian was nearby, playing poker with a wino. He had already won most of the man's pitiful possessions.

Dawn's left hand was in the sky, and with it Spiff found courage. He looked around and said, "Can't we afford something better than *this*?"

Jubee indicated the latest "Albatross" headline: GANGLAND SEARCH FOR BOGUS BIG SHOT.

"You saw the headline. Every thug in town is after us."

Dud had his own tale of woe. "They shot up my relative's house so bad it looks like a sieve. I heard he's in Havana and still running."

"We've got friends here," Spiff said, "lots of friends."

"We can't endanger them," Jubee said. "All we can do is hide out for a few weeks, somehow get some money, and then leave town." He began to rummage in the trunk.

"What are you doing?" asked Dud.

Jubee began putting on some clothes. "I've got to say goodbye to Margaret. I just can't leave her there."

"Where are you saying it?"

"At the Millionaires Club. I've invited her to lunch."

Spiff was aghast. "Are you crazy? You can't go back there. And you certainly can't show up with Margaret. They don't allow women in the dining room."

Jubee smiled wanly. "I promised her she could eat there, and I'm not going back on my word. I'll find a way. Stay here and guard the trunk."

And newly-clothed, he left.

*　*　*　*　*

Noon found Jubee hiding behind a potted plant in the foyer of the Millionaires Club. He checked his watch, then looked over at the concierge, who was talking on the phone. The boy then carefully edged his way into the lounge. It was filled with the usual assortment of slumbering millionaires. He looked at them with mild disgust, then crouched down to the first figure and whispered in his ear:

"It's time — to vote — Republican."

The creature stirred uneasily. Jubee continued on to more.

"The country's in danger. You've got — to vote — Republican."

"The Democrats are holding sway, you've got to vote and save the day."

"Labor unions are getting strong. Your vote today will right this wrong."

"If the Democrats win, they'll take all that you've got. Including your mistress, and hundred-foot yacht."

He continued on throughout the room.

"It's time — to vote — Republican."

"It's time — to vote — Republican."

Four of the first figures came awake.

"It's time — to vote — Republican."

"We hear the clarion call."

"The Democrats are at the gates."

"What we hold dear could fall."

The entire room was coming alive as more and more began to sing "It's Time to Vote Republican," a song extolling the virtues of the Grand Old Party. It warned of the dangers the country faced from Democrats, Socialists,

"I LIKE BEING WHERE I'M NOT SUPPOSED TO BE," SAID MARGARET.

THE END OF A WONDERFUL ERA

Communists, anarchists, atheists, free-thinkers, anti-vivisectionists, ecumenical conferences, and women who bob their hair. Many were ringing for their cars.

The automobile board behind the desk lit up. A hundred lights were flashing, and the astonished concierge began speaking into a tube. Chauffeurs ran out from an adjacent doorway, and limousines began appearing on the drive. The lounge was quickly emptied, some members pausing only to remove old blunderbusses off the wall.

Margaret appeared in the entryway as the concierge was frantically helping the millionaires into their cars. Jubee signaled surreptitiously and ushered her down the hall into the dining room. He bolted the door behind them.

"I'm sure glad you came," he said.

"My," she replied. "I've never seen such activity."

"Well, it needn't bother us. Let's sit over by the window." They walked across the room as a black waiter came out of the kitchen door. He did a double take, then smiled and advanced.

The sun was golden in the room. The silverware was bright, laid out in strict precision, and the linens had been lovingly embroidered by nuns in cells that overlooked old churchyards. The goblets shone impeccably, and the flowers were so kissed by cherubs they spoke of paradise.

Jubee was effusive. He had once memorized a poem for extra credit, and he felt it would be useful now. He began by passing her the rolls.

"Here with a Loaf of Bread beneath the Bough…"

She asked him for the butter.

"A Flask of Wine, a Book of Verse — and Thou."

She said she preferred a Pepsi.

"Beside me Singing in the Wilderness."

"Didn't you like John McCormack? You never did tell me."

The moment had passed, plus he'd forgotten the last line anyway.

An hour later they were having dessert.

"I like being here," Margaret said. "I like being where I'm not supposed to be."

The Wonderful Edison Time Machine

"Someday women will have *all* their rights," Jubee offered.

"You must be very important to have pulled this off."

"That's just it…" the boy replied. "I'm too important. That is, I mean, I've got to say goodbye. A friend of mine wants me to go with him to search for the Ark of the Covenant, and the Holy Grail, and even the Capshaw Diamond."

"A friend of yours. Do I know him?"

"No. He's from Indiana. He's an archaeologist."

"Will you come back?" the girl asked.

"Well, it's ever so dangerous, snakes and pits and everything. But I'm sure I'll see you again…someday."

"Well, you'd better. I like you…I like you a lot."

Jubee felt a quickening in his stomach. "What will you do?"

"Mom and Dad want me to go with them to Lord Doomsbury's villa in Antibes," she replied. "The Wizzer's ready to send to New York, but I don't know. I read that hard times are coming, and maybe there's something I can do to help."

Jubee put her hand in his. "Whatever you do, wherever you go, know that you're a fine woman. Don't ever get discouraged. Don't ever retreat…into a house…and close your eyes to the world."

"Meeting you has changed things. I…" She looked down upon his hand and tightened hers. "Do be careful."

The waiter came over with a bill for him to sign. Jubee sighed.

"Do you have fifty cents I can leave as a tip? I left my change in my other pants."

Margaret held back tears and laughed: "You millionaires are all alike. You never carry change."

She put the money down and they rose to leave.

*   *   *   *   *

The days had turned cold and blustery. One afternoon Spiff, dressed sparsely, stood in front of a proud sign announcing "Future Site of Flint

THE END OF A WONDERFUL ERA

Technical College — A School for Everyone." He kept his hands in his pockets and watched as in the distance men cleared land.

Dud, scruffy, was in a poorer part of town. He was looking at a faded "Dud's Suds" poster. A workman entered and pasted over a new sign: "Governor Franklin D. Roosevelt of New York State speaking at the IMA Auditorium Nov. 9." He shuffled off.

Downtown Flint was still a busy place, with throngs of shoppers, restaurant patrons and early theater crowds. Packards, Buicks and La Salles vied loftily for curb space, while spritely Model A's and Chevrolets chased merrily between them. Wizzer Stove-Bolt Sixes, Durants and old Flints chugged loyally along and hoped no one would equate them with the Model T's.

Some pedestrians had stopped to see four sidewalk singers. They were, of course, our heroes. Jubee, Lucian and Dud were all in black face, while Spiff was painted white, and the song they sang was "Smiles":

"There are smiles that make you happy,

There are smiles that make you sad…"

Dud played a squeezebox and Jubee a cheap violin in rough accordance with how the music had been written, and Spiff and Lucian tap-danced. If there were any tears among the greasepaint, no one noticed, and when the song concluded, some coins were tossed into their cap. The people went about their way, and someone took their picture.

*　*　*　*　*

It was raining lightly in the Flint railway yards, and new puddles were being splashed into existence. It was close to midnight, and freight cars and locomotives huddled morosely, cast in long shadows from the faint light of a distant marshaling yard. Three men were pushing the new Wizzer Playboy into a boxcar. David, Derby and Margaret stood nearby, as did Meadowcroft and Imogene, who were holding hands. With a sliding sound, the boxcar door was shut.

Imogene, Margaret and David then crossed over several tracks. Music and

THE WONDERFUL EDISON TIME MACHINE

voices drifted to them. Ahead was a private railway car, its rear platform hung with decorations and its windows filled with lights. They entered to a blast of jazz. The silly people had been transferred here — the women filled with emptiness, the men who seemed to float on air — and the party was as strong as ever. Their parents greeted them, and they kissed goodbye. Imogene did the same with the British lord, whose face was filled with vagueness. The car then lurched, and with a few last hugs and waves, the children left.

They watched with their umbrellas as the cars began to move. Two beautiful young people came out onto the platform and intertwined in love and wine and toasted mirthfully the unseen legions of the dead who were to come, until the car receded and was lost, taking with it the last of the Roaring Twenties.

CHAPTER THIRTY-ONE

IT WAS THE WORST OF TIMES

Meanwhile, the boys had left what lice they could behind, and moved into a religious mission. The sheets were cleaner there, and if one dropped the soap in the shower, it could more safely be retrieved. Other bathroom amenities were sometimes sparse, but there was no end of religious tracts that proved useful in their stead. The place was poor, but it offered much; but you had to die to get it. An amenable general was in charge, and no matter how threadbare you were, he would always inquire about your soul. The boys felt he would be cashiered out of any regular army, but the mush they served was good, provided you did not look too closely at the raisins, and there was plenty of it. To get it you had to attend evening service. Dud and Spiff were always saved on schedule, but Jubee found it irritating.

On this night rows of down-and-outers were singing "I Love to Tell The Story":

"I love to tell the Story,
'Twill be my theme in Glory
To tell the old, old Story
Of Jesus and His love."

The three boys were sitting so far back they were practically outside. The song ended. Jubee was bitter.

"It's bad enough to be broke. Now I have to sing Christian hymns."

The Wonderful Edison Time Machine

Dud was at the end of his rope.

"Why don't you tell them how you got your name, Jubee? Then maybe you won't have to."

"Whaddaya mean? My name *is* Jubee. I took it 'cause I like the candy."

"You took it because Stuttering Stella called you a 'Jew boy' in the sixth grade, and you wanted everybody to think she said 'Jubee,' so you've been eating Jujubes ever since, and I don't think you even like them."

"That's not true," cried Jubee, hitting Dud. "You *know* that's not true!"

They went struggling to the floor. Jubee's eyes were red with tears when Spiff managed to part them.

"Lay off, you guys," he commanded. "*I'm* the one who's stuck in an era where there aren't any civil rights."

The boys sat down. Then Lucian appeared, dressed as a mission officer. He smiled piously and extended a long pole with a collection box at the end. Jubee went berserk.

* * * * *

Later it was bedtime. Spiff and Lucian were asleep together. Dud was sitting on his bed, dejected. Jubee returned from the washroom and offered Dud his case of Jujubes. The boy took a few, pressed Jubee on his thigh, and they turned in.

* * * * *

Thread Lake was dreary and restless on a day both sullen and forlorn. The moored boats rose and fell on the water with loosed cordage and flapping sail. The summer people all had fled, and nature seemed on hold.

Jubee was standing by the magic fountain inside the Willoughby mansion. It was as dry as any in old Pompeii. The house seemed to echo of the Never-Ending Party, yet every sound was muffled. He went down the stairs. All the furniture was covered. Outside a gardener was raking leaves. Jubee asked him a question which the wind appropriated. The man shook his head, and the boy continued on.

JUBEE WAS READING TO HIS LITTLE BROTHER WHILE RAIN SQUALLS
THRASHED THE WINDOWPANE OUTSIDE.

It Was the Worst of Times

*   *   *   *   *

Evening closed in on their now small world and held them tightly in a ball of warmth as rain squalls thrashed the windowpane that kept the darkness out.

Jubee was reading a storybook to Lucian, who was so familiar with the lines that they repeated them together:

Wicked Willie

"My name is Wicked Willie,
I'm a terror, understand -
A pirate on the water
And a savage on the land.

"I can wade out in the occan
And sink a mighty fleet;
I can corner up an army
And stamp it with my feet."

"Dr. Hooey gave me this book for winning the contest," the little boy said with satisfaction, as he always did soon after the poem began.

Jubee had never dared ask what the contest was about, but it involved an "Alternative Religions" class and the purchase of a Quetzalcoatl feathered serpent cloak and an obsidian sacrificial knife from a mail-order firm in Tikal. An immense weariness engulfed him, but he continued gamely on.

"The other night I took a boat
And sailed to Galipup
And captured twenty elephants
Before the sun was up."

Lucian had closed his eyes and was already on the high seas, sword in hand.

THE WONDERFUL EDISON TIME MACHINE

"I'll tell you what — in Africa
I had an awful fight
With fifty wild orangutans
But I came out all right —"

The lad had little conception of how much fifty was, but he conjured up enough orangutans to make him look a hero.

"I tied a knot in all their tails
And hung them on a pole
And carried them to Jericho
And dumped them in a hole.

"I could fight the King of Cuba
And the sheriff of Japan;
I could bottle up Goliath
In an old tomato can."

Lucian had seen the King of Cuba on TV in his home that now seemed far away, and he quickly overcame the man in green fatigues and pulled his bushy beard. Goliath he also knew about, and brought him down as well. But now the youth was on uncharted seas, and the words were barely heard.

"I could toss a team of horses up
And land them in Peru —
It's hard to think of anything
I really couldn't do."

Jubee read the last lines so softly an angel would have strained to hear:

"My name is Wicked Willie
I'm a terror, understand —
Just tell them I am coming
And get out the city band!"

It Was the Worst of Times

...and he, too, drifted off to sleep.

*   *   *   *   *

The photograph of the kids performing "Smiles" might not have won any awards, but it was highly interesting to *some* people, and passed from hand to hand.

A few nights later the kids were loaded down with props as they made their way along the thoroughfares of Flint. Across the street the three bankers were holding out tin cups. They saw the boys, and one of them fished out a nickel and headed for a phone.

The kids continued on, oblivious. They passed four men who were selling Ovaltine. Behind them was a mountain of the stuff. One man compared them to a photograph.

Further on, the Ossified chairman emerged from his town car. He was greeted by Mayor McKeighan and the two hobos. All of them lit torches and turned down the street as the four anarchists passed like shadows in the background. No sooner did they disappear than the kids appeared and turned *up* the street.

Nearby, the concierge with Thaddeus in tow rounded a corner and almost collided with the Prohibition agent. They were joined by the Grand Pistachio, Meddlesome, Gatsby and his lady friend, still in her soiled wedding dress, the cannibal king, and those members of the Millionaires Club who were still ambulatory. All were carrying torches. Last to join were Fred and Flora Flummox, who dropped down in a basket from the sky. They were much the worse for wear, and had arrows sticking out, but they joined with the others who spread out in grim determination.

Just blocks away the kids had set up shop and were performing "Uncle Tom's Cabin" to a few stragglers and youths who'd been stood up. A makeshift bed had been provided, and Spiff was Little Eva, dying from some nineteenth century malady that left one looking better dead. Jubee was Uncle Tom, kneeling by her bedside, a fuzzy whitened wig upon his head, his body wracked with sobs. Dud, still dressed as Simon Legree, handled a rope that dangled Lucian, dressed as an angel and holding a halo, above the scene.

"Where do you suppose new Jerusalem is, Uncle Tom?" croaked Spiff, wishing he weren't so perilously close to Dud, since they'd had beans for supper.

"O, up in the clouds, Miss Eva," said Jubee, using his third finger to point skyward. Spiff got the message.

"Then I think I see it," said Spiff, using *his* third finger to direct Jubee's attention. "Look in those clouds! — they look like great gates of pearl, and you can see beyond them — far, far off. I'm going there."

"Where, Miss Eva?" blubbered Jubee, wiping his nose on the quilt.

"To the spirits bright, Tom; *I'm going* — oh! Love, — joy, — peace!"

Suddenly a dog barked. Startled, Dud looked up and saw they were confronted by their adversaries. He dropped Lucian, who landed squarely on Little Eva's private parts. *Squish*!

"Damn," said Dud.

"Ouch," said Spiff.

"Ooof," said Lucian.

"Run," said Jubee.

Spiff was apprehended, but Dud hit his attacker with their "Next Week EAST LYNNE" sign. In the ensuing melee several millionaires were set on fire, and only the hobos knew how to put it out. Amid the confusion, the thespians took off.

Thaddeus hadn't been so excited since he'd tracked down Sacco and Vanzetti. The dog had broken free from the concierge and bounded ahead of the mob. He had now reached a deserted corner and was sniffing broadly. He knew his quarry wasn't far.

Ahead was a Hoover Vacuum Cleaner store with several models in its windows. Placards stating "Housewives Vote Hoover Best" were on a fence, and a covered trash bin lay nearby. Thaddeus loped over and placed his front

THE KIDS WERE PERFORMING UNCLE TOM'S CABIN IN THE DOWNTOWN STREETS OF FLINT.

paws high on it, his tail a happy blur. Jubee raised the lid and held out a partially torn sign: "Vote Hoover." Satisfied, the dog withdrew.

But the other men had seen him. "There they are!" they cried, and the boys jumped out and continued running.

More joined in from side streets, and the mob was closer now. Ahead of the boys were broad steps leading to a Gothic church. Breathless, Jubee had an idea.

"Follow me. This always works, at least in France."

They reached the steps. Jubee assumed a patriarchal stance, finger pointed heavenward. Dud pulled his sweater over his forehead and held the infant Lucian, the halo above his head. Spiff kneeled and held in offering the golden case of Jujubes. The mob stopped, their torches blazing.

"This is hallowed Christian ground," intoned Jubee, sternly, "and I claim *sanctuary*."

The boy looked at them smugly. The mob considered briefly and then surged forward. A Flint sanitation cart was pulled up and the boys were tossed inside.

"Maybe it's because I'm Jewish," mused Jubee, as they were hauled away.

The mob escorted them with shouts and curses up a cobblestone street toward the Old Mill Bakery, whose ponderous creaking sails dominated a hilltop. Beside it at a crazy angle was a gibbet that had four nooses, the last a smaller one. The kids looked on, defiantly. Suddenly two gangster cars blocked an intersection, and gunmen scrambled out.

"Slugsy wants those guys!" they cried, and shot out all four street lamps. New ones dropped down, but not in time to stop hysteria. In the ensuing uproar more millionaires were singed, as the hobos were played out, and Thaddeus was stepped on. But amid the pandemonium, the boys escaped for good.

CHAPTER THIRTY-TWO

THE SET MAKER

The Flint Foreign Legion recruiting office apparently had standards, for the following day all four boys were kicked out of it. The sergeant *had* said that Dud reminded him of a camel he'd once owned, but that was not enough. Wearily, they dusted themselves off.

"That was our last hope," lamented Jubee.

"What do we do now?" asked Spiff.

"Kill ourselves," said Jubee.

Lucian had other ideas. "Speak for yourself. I'm going to be adopted by a *rich* lady."

They ignored him and turned onto Saginaw.

"Maybe I'll go to Hollywood and see Ayn Rand," said Jubee. "She's out there, you know."

"If she's beautiful, I'll go with you," said Dud.

Spiff reflected briefly that L. Ron Hubbard might be out there somewhere, too, but then he spoke bitterly. "You know what day this is, don't you? November second. In ten hours we're supposed to return to 1991."

"You don't have to remind me," said Jubee.

"Hey, *look*," cried Dud excitedly. They were passing the Capitol Theater, which was showing "The Cocoanuts." In front was a hinged sign: "TODAY AT MATINEE — THE FOUR MARX BROTHERS — IN PERSON."

"*The Marx Brothers!*" Dud exclaimed. "All four of them. Even *Zeppo*.

THE SET MAKER

What a chance to see them."

"And what will we use for money?" Jubee asked.

"We've got five dollars left," his friend replied. "That's enough for tickets *and* refreshments."

"That's our bus fare out of town," protested Spiff.

"We'll worry about that later," Dud said, pulling them toward the box office. "This is a chance to see the Marx Brothers in *real life*." And without further ado, they joined the growing line.

Later on, the boys were munching on a host of goodies and watching the newsreel. It left them cold that Mussolini was draining the Pontine Marshes, but then came a sonorous voice:

"DEARBORN, MICHIGAN, Monday, October 21. Thomas Alva Edison, the world's greatest inventor, tonight recreated before a handful of distinguished guests his first successful illumination of an incandescent light bulb." The newsreel showed Thomas Edison and Henry Ford passing into a plain, white-columned structure.

"Wow," said Jubee. "That's the guy who invented our Time Machine."

"The occasion was the official opening of Henry Ford's new Greenfield Village, a vast complex of buildings designed to show how Americans lived in the past.

"Foremost among the exhibits is Edison's own laboratory. In rare, historic scenes, Edison is here shown conducting his long-time friend, the world's greatest automobile manufacturer, through the reconstructed building that has seen some 1,093 scientific discoveries during its half-century of existence." The newsreel camera swept the laboratory, revealing a *1910 Edison Time Machine!*

"A TIME MACHINE," the boys cried out in unison, and tumbled out of the theater. Only Lucian was distraught. "I want to see *Curly*," he whined.

Jubee was overwhelmed with excitement. "Edison must have built *two* Time Machines."

"So all we have to do is get to *that* one," Dud enthused.

THE WONDERFUL EDISON TIME MACHINE

"That wouldn't do any good," said Spiff. "That's a *different* machine. It's not the one we used in 1991."

"Yes, it is," cried Jubee. "It *has* to be. Don't you see? We've changed history. Just by our being here, the Flint of 1991 *is changed*."

"You mean it's *better* now?" asked Dud.

"It can't be any worse," said Spiff.

Jubee had an explanation. "At least the Time Machine's been changed. It's no longer the one we used in 1991. That one was destroyed. There's now a *different* Time Machine in a new and different 1991. It's now the one in Edison's lab."

"How do you figure that?" said Spiff.

"Because we're *here*, in 1929. And we came here in a Time Machine. If *one* of the Time Machines was destroyed, so it couldn't have sent us, then it's *got* to be the other one."

"So how did it get to your place from the lab?" said Spiff, who always felt safer being fully informed.

"Who knows? Who cares? It just got there, that's all. And," he said triumphantly, "it's going to take us back to 1991 *tonight!*"

*　　*　　*　　*　　*

A short time later the boys were on Dixie Highway outside Flint, attempting to hitchhike.

"No one wants to pick up four kids," said Spiff.

"Maybe we could leave Lucifer behind," volunteered Dud.

"No. He'd be sure to become a Nazi," retorted Jubee.

Lucian knew this was no compliment, and kicked his brother in the shin. Jubee raised his pant leg in concern.

"That's it," said Dud, lighting up. "Roll up your pant leg like in that old movie we saw."

"Never mind," said Spiff. "I think this truck is stopping."

An older truck pulled up, with two men in the cab.

SUDDENLY A FLOOD OF DAZZLING LIGHT ILLUMINATED THE PIT.

THE SET MAKER

"We're headed for Detroit," said one. "The little kid can ride in front, but the rest of you will have to climb in back."

"Gee, thanks; swell; let's go," said the kids in chorus as they raced to the back, not seeing the "King Guano" sign on its side, or Lucian sticking his tongue out at them.

Several hours later they were in a run-down section of Detroit. Lucian was waving goodbye to the driver as the boys regrouped. The older ones were filthy.

"Now we know what guano is," acknowledged Spiff.

"*I'm hungry*," announced Lucian.

"All I've got left is half a box of Jujubes," said Jubee, removing his gold box.

"We can do better than that," said Spiff, pointing to a nearby line of unemployed, shambling men. "There's a soup kitchen."

Once inside, the boys acquired trays, each with a bowl and spoon. Jubee, black with grime, his hair long and partly covered by his cap, was mouthing the last of his Jujubes. As he pushed his tray forward, he saw Margaret handing out rolls.

He stared at her, transfixed, and hid the box of candy behind him. Margaret looked at the strange, disheveled young man and laughed, saying to her sister, who was serving soup, "I've made a conquest."

She extended a roll to him, and the youth fell back. She held up a quarter in her other hand, and Jubee moved away.

THE WONDERFUL EDISON TIME MACHINE

Margaret then came around the counter and extended him the roll. Sheepishly, he accepted it. She brought around his other hand to give him the coin. She found the box of Jujubes. She caressed the box and looked at him in disbelief. She ran her hand up his arm and touched his face. Then she touched her own.

"YOU?" she said.

Jubee nodded in embarrassment, the roll held close to his mouth. It was a moment for eternity.

Except for Lucian, who had no use for reverie.

"Hey! Let's get this line moving," he complained. "My soup is getting cold."

A short time later, Spiff, Dud and Lucian, now all cleaned up, were standing outside a tailor shop. Inside, one of Slugsy's gangsters was accepting the weekly payoff money from the elderly tailor and his sad, onlooking wife. He made a check mark in his notebook then, turning to go, recognized the kids. He stopped to listen, just as Jubee sprinted up.

"Margaret's given us some money, too. So we can take a cab to Greenfield Village. It's only a few miles from here. And Edison's laboratory is just inside." They began to walk away. "All we have to do is be there by eleven."

The gangster wrote the information down.

After a few steps, Dud stopped the group. "What'll we do until then? It's getting dark."

Spiff interjected. "I want to go off somewhere. Just for a little while…to be by myself."

"It's that gold coin, isn't it?" said Jubee. The one your grandfather had. I'm sorry, Spiff; I really am."

"It's okay," his black friend replied. "I just want to be alone. I'll meet you back here in plenty of time." He turned away as Jubee looked at him with concern.

*   *   *   *   *

Within a few blocks Spiff found himself on a forgotten street that even the hopeless had abandoned. Its ancient, weathered buildings leaned precariously, and bore worn, faded dates like tombstones in a cemetery. There was but one sign of life, a patch of light emanating from a filthy pawnshop window. He stopped and looked inside.

In its distant recess, an elderly proprietor was counting the day's receipts. He tucked a few gold coins in his vest, closed the door of his safe, and prepared to leave.

Spiff spied several bricks at the bottom of a nearby excavation pit. He jumped in, picked one up, and crouched beside the rim. The old man locked his shop and moved on down the street.

Conflicting emotions raged within the boy, and his tortured fingers clasped and unclasped the brick. The proprietor turned a corner and disappeared. Despairing, Spiff hung down his head.

Suddenly cries rang out. "There they are. OVER THERE!"

There came the sound of running steps, then police whistles and shots. Two black men leaped into the pit and returned the fire. The smaller of them said, "The docks are two blocks away. It'll be dark in a minute. We can make it."

"There's too many of them," the larger man said. "And I've no bullets left."

Beams of light swept the street and reached the pit. The larger man saw Spiff and yanked the boy upright.

"I'VE GOT A KID HERE. STOP YOUR SHOOTING."

The shots intensified. Puffs of dirt exploded beside them.

"C'mon!" the larger man said. "We'll use him as a shield."

"NO!" cried the smaller man, striking the larger one. The man ran off, and more shots rang out. The smaller man, crossed in the beams of light, was hit. He toppled backward, and Spiff moved to him.

"Hey, kid," the dying man said. "My right pocket. Deep!"

Spiff felt in the pocket and extracted a gold coin.

"It's all I have. I don't want them to get it. *Now run!*"

Spiff looked over the rim. Scores of police were running up. He rose to flee, then staggered back as shots rang out anew.

THE WONDERFUL EDISON TIME MACHINE

Suddenly a flood of blazing light illuminated the pit. A pair of immaculate shoes appeared in the dirt at the pit's rim, only inches from Spiff's face. They were golden shoes, diamond shoes, shoes all colors of the rainbow. A thousand kingdoms could not pay their ransom. Spiff lifted his eyes and gazed transfixed into the blinding glory of — The Set Maker.

The figure looked in fury at the dead man in the pit. From his robes of swirling night he pulled a gossamer cloth embedded with jewels. Angrily he rent the veil in two. From it dropped a single stone, which landed by the body and winked out. In the background his hooded followers were dismantling the buildings revealing false fronts and temporary scaffolding. The police were frozen in mid-flight. Two of the followers picked up the phantom spirit of the dead man and carried it away.

The Set Maker then turned to look at Spiff. In terror beyond meaning, the youth bolted and ran — past the lighted pit, past the statues of the police, past the skeletons of the buildings which were being rudely carted off — out into the night.

The police arrived and flashed their lights.

"It's him, all right. Big Jim Birdsong! He'll never rob another payroll truck."

"Big Jim Birdsong. Dead at last!"

Their voices grew fainter. "You think he gave that kid something?" inquired one. "Naw! What would *he* have to give?" replied another.

Spiff ran down now rain-washed streets as if all Hell were after him. Finally he saw a circle of light and his three friends waiting for him beneath a lamp post.

"Jesus Christ! Where have you been?" said Jubee. "We've hardly time to make it."

They jumped into the cab, and Spiff looked out the beaded window as it pulled away. Later he fingered his jacket and found the bullet hole, which was only inches from his heart.

CHAPTER THIRTY-THREE

GREENFIELD VILLAGE

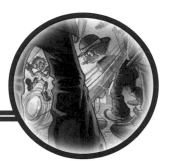

Greenfield Village was both dark and deserted when the boys arrived. Vague forms of buildings stood within, and all was very still. They were immediately confronted by a high fence. Dud and Spiff helped Jubee reach the top, while Lucian walked through the open gate and helped his brother down. Dud lifted Spiff up, then crossed over himself. They all crouched down and looked around.

"Don't let anybody see us," Jubee whispered. "We'll break into the lab a few minutes before eleven. That way, even if we set off an alarm, we'll be gone before anyone can come."

They held hands apprehensively and advanced down a street still wet and glistening from the rain. They stopped in front of a sign: "The Edison Institute — Menlo Park Laboratory."

"This is it," said Jubee.

Then they froze. Slugsy and his gang were just ahead of them, coming to a stop. The gangster took a lighted yo-yo from his pocket and proceeded to use it. The other mobsters did the same.

Slugsy, four ferocious feet of fiendness, approached the trembling boys and began to circle them, deftly demonstrating his latest yo-yo skills. Lucian took up the challenge and began to follow him, the gangster now walking backward and taunting the boy with every stride. The encirclement was almost complete, when Slugsy fouled up. He had lost. Everyone, without exception, glared at Lucian.

THE WONDERFUL EDISON TIME MACHINE

The gangsters snapped their machine guns. The boys were about to die. "This is it," said Jubee.

Suddenly there came a calm, authoritative voice.

"Mr. Bennett, if you please."

It came from a tall, shadowed figure on the Victorian porch of the Edison Institute. As if by magic, a hundred men with guns appeared. They dropped from trees, they leaned from windows, they took aim from rooftops and chimneys, and even sprang from manholes. More appeared in quick-step from around a corner, and the gangsters dropped their guns and fled.

"A few of my private security force, Mr. Edison," said the voice. "I usually use them against labor agitators."

"So I've heard," said Edison, some disapproval in his voice. "Still, I'm glad they're here. I was worried for a moment."

The two men stepped down from the porch, and Thomas Edison, with hand extended, walked over to the boys.

"We've been expecting you," he said.

"EXPECTING US?"

"Some time ago I noticed that my Time Machine was set to return someone to the future on November second. I was curious as to who it was. But first, allow me to present my good friend, Henry Ford."

"GOSH!" the boys responded.

"You mean you *know* your Time Machine works?" Jubee said.

"I've always known it worked."

"Then why didn't you ever use it?" Dud said.

"I've never been interested in the past," the inventor replied. "Only in the future. In the progress of mankind. Tell me, how are things in 1991?"

"There are a lot of problems," Dud acknowledged. "But we still like your light bulb."

Edison chuckled. "Well, there's always going to be problems. That's what makes life interesting."

EVERYONE, WITHOUT EXCEPTION, GLARED AT LUCIAN, WHO HAD WON THE CONTEST.

GREENFIELD VILLAGE

"We had another world war," said Jubee. "An awful lot of people died. And a president that everybody liked was shot. 1991 could stand improvement. That's why we came here. To make our world better."

Ford looked at Spiff. "And are your people happy, son?"

Spiff began to cry.

"Our time is running short," warned Edison hastily. "Come, Henry, I somehow feel you don't believe in Time Machines."

The two men shepherded the boys into the lab, Ford's arm around Spiff's shoulders. Inside, they stood before the Time Machine. Jubee looked up. Margaret was standing in the doorway. She had believed him after all.

Edison looked at his watch. "In just a minute, maybe two."

Suddenly Jubee stepped aside. His legs were like water, and it was all he could do to stand. "I'm not going back," he stammered. "I'm staying here."

"Why?" gasped Spiff and Dud.

"I want to stay and fight," he said. "Slugsy's gone and there's a depression coming on. It's not enough to have saved the company. We've got to change, change as a nation. Somewhere along the line we got lazy. We thought the world owed us a living, but it doesn't. Life's *not* a never-ending party. We've got to *work*.

"I've been thinking," he said with growing confidence. "We shouldn't fight the Japanese. They're our friends, and they got ahead of us by working harder. We should stop complaining and do the same. We can build good cars, too. It's up to *us* to bring prosperity back."

"We'll stay, too," cried Dud.

"You can't," said Jubee. "Someone has to take Lucian back." The little boy ran over and hugged his brother. "The folks might miss him. And if you *go* back, you can *come* back. Any time. We can have more adventures together."

The Time Machine, a thousand minarets of light, was beginning to unfold like a view of Cairo from the citadel when Saladin was king.

THE WONDERFUL EDISON TIME MACHINE

"Go on," the boy continued. "If we're successful, I'll be waiting for you in a great new 1991."

"What if you die in the meantime?" said Spiff, a new tear forming in his eye.

"If there's a God in heaven, I'll be there."

The three boys moved within the multi-colored sphere. The machine began to levitate. Henry Ford looked on in disbelief.

"Goodbye, Mr. Edison," said Spiff. "Thanks for all your help."

"Goodbye, Mr. Ford," said Dud. "Don't let anyone name a car after your son."

In a final burst of light, the boys disappeared. The Time Machine settled back to earth, and the lab was quiet again.

"I somehow feel the future is in good hands," said Tom Edison. And Henry Ford agreed.

Jubee walked across the room and kissed Margaret with all the love his young heart could provide.

CHAPTER THIRTY-FOUR

HOME AGAIN

The Time Machine had just returned the boys to 1991. They gazed around the room. It wasn't changed. They moved to the door. It had been splintered by an axe. Dud and Spiff looked at each other in despair.

Cautiously, they opened the door. There was no sound in the shrouded hallway. Holding onto one another, they moved down the dusty stairs and peered outside. The lawn was overgrown, and the mansion was completely dark.

"Nothing's changed," cried Spiff bitterly.

But the night wind rustled the trees with a celestial sigh, and a sound came, although they did not hear.

"I love to tell the Story…" and it was among the dry leaves scattered on the grass.

"'Twill be my theme in Glory…" and it wound among the eaves and cupolas.

"To tell the old, old Story…" and it cooled the foreheads of the three young boys, although they did not feel.

"Of Jesus and His love," and they were blessed by God, although they did not know.

And then a strange thing happened. Faintly, as if from far away, there came to them the tinkling notes of "The Japanese Sandman." As it increased, a mellow light appeared within the house, and soon it was aglow. People streamed from the terrace doors as the fountains sprang to life, and there were people waving from the pool.

THE WONDERFUL EDISON TIME MACHINE

The three boys raced around the front. The doors were open, and people were within. The boys rushed in and mounted the staircase.

Waiting for them beside the magic fountain were Jubee, in a tux, and Margaret, both now in their seventies. The boys stopped on the top stair, unsure. Jubee, cane in hand, took a Jujube from a gold box and popped it in his mouth. Then to cheers that rang the hall, they rushed together and embraced.

Lucian happily splashed a glass among the fountain's silver spigots. The choices now were healthful, and he liked the grape juice best. Suddenly there came the melodic sound of an automobile horn.

The crowd parted as the five of them descended the staircase. Outside, the Flint Technical College band, a handsome assortment of all races, was playing a rousing rendition of "The Japanese Sandman." They were ably assisted by a smartly-uniformed Central High School band, and one of renown from the local campus of the University of Michigan.

A shimmering new Wizzer convertible was circling the drive. They all climbed in and, with a dignity due to years of having money, Jubee settled down.

SPLAT!!

He held up a whoopee cushion.

"GOD DAMN IT, LUCIAN," he said.

"That's *Lucifer*," the little boy replied.

The car took off as everyone waved goodbye. It slowed at a nearby intersection. Across the street was a large billboard that showed a man standing behind a new car and saying, "I'm taking a Wizz." Below were the words, "The All-New Wizzer for 1992." Below the sign was a low collection of buildings surrounded by a fence. It also had a sign: "Krockashita and Sons — Gardeners and Landscape Architects — Since 1929."

The car turned right and accelerated as a child's voice was heard.

"Do you remember 'Wicked Willie?'"

"I sure do," said an older one, and they repeated it together.

HOME AGAIN

"My name is Wicked Willie
I'm a terror, understand —
Just tell them I am coming
And get out the city band!"

And then in front of them, rising in the distance like a shower of jewels, was the Emerald City of Oz. As the car disappeared down the road, it passed a highway sign:

FLINT, MICHIGAN — AUTOMOBILE CAPITAL OF THE WORLD.

And that is the last we see for this time of our Central High School heroes and the intrepid citizens of the great metropolis of Flint, except for Spiff, whose hands that very evening returned the gold coin to the family album. He noticed that the epitaph now read:

"Big Jim Birdsong, 1883-1929."

The boy stared long and hard at the faded dates, then bowed his head and softly closed the book.

THE END

A Special Note

It is a true story that in Flint in 1929 there were three high-ranking bank officials who were embezzling bank funds to speculate in the stock market. When the Crash came, they could not return the money. All three went to prison, and one died there. The bank was narrowly saved due to the fact that its owner had sufficient funds to replace the depositors' money. Jubee knew this and was able to take advantage of it.

The newsreel mentioned in Chapter 32 is factual. Thomas Edison did reenact his original illumination of an electric light bulb at Greenfield Village on October 21, 1929, and Henry Ford was in attendance. The author asks his readers as a matter of faith to believe there was a wonderful Edison Time Machine in the background.

The character Harry Bennett actually lived, and from 1927 until 1945 he was Henry Ford's chief aide and hatchet man. Head of Ford Service, the world's largest private army, he cowed Ford employees and battled the United Auto Workers in a series of confrontations culminating in a bloody strike and settlement in 1941. When Henry Ford II succeeded his grandfather as company president in 1945, his first act was to fire Bennett, after which he sacked, demoted or transferred a thousand of Bennett's men.

The remainder of Bennett's 87 years were spent in Nevada and California. His Michigan castle, designed by Ford and Bennett with the enthusiasm of small boys fashioning a robbers' lair or a pirates' nest and complete with turrets, tunnels, hidden rooms and a lion/tiger den, still broods over the Huron River Valley east of Ann Arbor. (Information courtesy of the noted Ford historian, Prof. David L. Lewis of the University of Michigan.)

So it is not surprising that Henry Ford had a portion of his private army with him at Greenfield Village the night of November 2, 1929, and was able to make short work of Slugsy and his gang.

Thomas Alva Edison died in 1931, Henry Ford died in 1947, and Harry Bennett died in 1979.

Some Special Thanks

To Ned Jordan and his trail-blazing Jordan Playboy automotive ads of the 1920s, in this case the most brilliant one of all: "Somewhere West of Laramie," which appeared in 1923. The ad's original illustration is reprinted on the next page.

To Harriet Beecher Stowe for her historic and deeply moving novel "Uncle Tom's Cabin," as well as the line, "The moored boats rose and fell on the water with loosed cordage and flapping sail," which I used in Chapter 31.

To Edward Fitzgerald and his famous translation of Quatrain XI from "The Rubiyat of Omar Khayyam," as well as the line, "When dawn's left hand was in the sky."

To Charlie Chaplin and his unforgettable ending to his much-beloved 1931 film masterpiece "City Lights."

To Margaret Mitchell and her gripping library scene at Twelve Oaks from the greatest of all Civil War dramas, "Gone With the Wind."

To Carl Barks, a long-time friend, who created Uncle Scrooge McDuck in late 1947. In the April 1946 issue of "Walt Disney's Comics and Stories," he included a character called Miss Swansdown Swoonsudden, and I liked the name so much I included it in Chapter 20.

To the many authors and artists of the past

MORE THANKS

who provided me with much-needed inspiration from such classic works as "Roger and Me," "Little Orphan Annie," "The Maltese Falcon," "The Great Gatsby," "The Music Man," "Duck Soup," "Public Enemy," "The Godfather," "My Fair Lady," the Indiana Jones films, Universal's great "Frankenstein" of 1931, and RKO's 1939 masterpiece "The Hunchback of Notre Dame."

To Leroy F. Jackson, author of "Rimskittle's Book" and the poem "Wicked Willie," published by Rand McNally & Company in 1926.

And to Jujubes, my favorite candy as a youth, because in the early 1940s a box would last through an entire double feature, a newsreel, a cartoon, a serial chapter, several previews, and a patriotic admonition to buy War Bonds.

*   *   *

Thanks also to Carly Mary Cady, who did an outstanding job both in researching and proofreading The Wonderful Edison Time Machine, and to Rudy Behlmer, a good friend, for contributing a number of worthwhile ideas and observations to my manuscript.

Thanks to the Howard Lowery Gallery in Burbank, California, for suggesting that Toby Bluth would make a fine illustrator for my story, and to Toby himself for doing such a magnificent job. Appreciation is extended as well to Steve Edrington of the Book Castle in Burbank for loaning the artist several 1928-1933 mail-order catalogues so that he might immerse himself in how objects and fashions appeared in the late 1920s.

Appreciation should be given to Helen Driscoll of the Fine Paper Company in Pasadena, California, for putting me in contact with C.W. Scott Rubel, who did an exceedingly fine job in designing the book. Recognition must also be given to Craig Woods of the Castle Press in Pasadena for his dedication and professionalism which contributed so greatly to the final quality and physical appearance of The Wonderful Edison Time Machine.

Professor David L. Lewis of the University of Michigan was most helpful in checking and correcting my manuscript in regard to the historical personages of Henry Ford and Harry Bennett. Much of the professor's lifetime has been devoted to researching and writing about the career of the great automotive industrialist, and there is no greater authority.

Mention should also be made of Mrs. Kathy Cochrane of Beaverton, Oregon, and her mother-in-law, Mrs. Frances E. Cochrane of King City, Oregon, for their continued encouragement while I wrote and polished The Wonderful Edison Time Machine. They were my very first fans, and hopefully not the last.

And finally, a sincere appreciation to Rev. Ed Bergen of Immanuel Lutheran Church in Crystal Lake, Illinois, for his never-ending interest in and enthusiasm for my project.

Malcolm Willits
Hollywood, California

GOODBYE, FAREWELL

They buried me with hollow words
on a day full of other days,
and left a gaping wound upon the earth.
None lingered to remember, and the sands of time
    moved quickly to efface
    all record of my resting place.

But I rose ere the last grieved loved one had departed,
    and I caressed those flowers not yet flung,
    and paused to touch the dampness of the tears
    that covered them.
Then I was gone, and while they left in chains,
    I now soared free.

How briefly did we live beneath the sun,
    pressing each day to our parched lips
    the liquors of a vintner unexcelled.
We let slip through our unheeding hands
    the bounty of the earth,
and spent the gold coins of our treasury
    for trifles

    I never knew what moved the earth
        or caused the seas to roll.
    I never knew what makes a flower
        or why death takes a toll.
    I never knew why comets blaze
        or why the wind runs free,
    I never knew how mountains rise,
        such things come hard for me.
    But I do know that roses bloom
        as part of God's domain,
    and that His son from outside time
        will someday come again.

If ever you should be where once I was,
    garlanded with flowers from some new summer day,
pause but a moment in my sylvan glade
to coolly drink from any spring that might be there,
    and then continue on.

Goodbye, farewell, my ship awaits
restless on an expectant sea, and I,
now breathless with new youth
race down the dawn-washed streets
and cry my welcome to the boisterous crew
who anchor only briefly in the star flood
    for tide of morn – and me.

MY SHIP AWAITS

And I shall grasp the railing and shout farewell
to all the sleeping world and those I've left behind
in warm sheets perfumed with my love. We were
as children playing in a long-neglected garden
whose ravaged gate and tumbled walls were raised
by titans. Clouds were our castles, and storm-bent trees
our dragons, the grass which covered all our pillows
in that place where twilight fell as a drowsy gift,
and those few stars which early shone, were jewels
set in an azure sky. If there were those who watched,
    we never knew.

The anchor weighs and the lines cut which
bound me fast to this fair world, and the
great sails swell with confidence. We move,
and swiftly pass through burnished shoals to
sun-flecked surf, where each new wave is crowned
with sprites that dip and vault like porpoises
and bid us on with spraying foam and laughter. We lift,
and winding sea gulls lead the way, but soon they eddy
far below as bracing air engulfs us. My home, my most
beloved home, my earth, my spot, my womb of incomparable
beauty, that cradle place which made of me a man
falls off and is lost in a shimmering sea.

I'll not forget thee, earth
    though ten trillion suns burn out,
    and all we know expands to nothingness,
your roads will be remembered.

All that live
    follow the great chord
which resonates throughout the universe
    and leads to God and home.

I wave, and my hands are young again. The wind
whips my open blouse, and my body is once more
hard bronze against the sun. The vast, unfathomable
ocean is soon obscured by clouds, and now the winds
blow gale-like in their rapture. Our stout ship
shudders, and the faithful helmsman struggles
with his course. We are tossed about like pilgrims
in a sudden squall on Galilee, but a far-off beacon
flashes through the heavens, and we know full well
we'll tether soon, in a tranquil town,
on the shores of Paradise.

When will I hear the pipes again
the soft-blown pipes of Pan.